Living in the Shadow

Living in the Shadow

Mark Beatleman

Second Edition

Hidden Brook Press
www.HiddenBrookPress.com
writers@HiddenBrookPress.com

Living in the Shadow
by Richard M. Grove

Cover Design – Richard M. Grove
Layout and Design – Richard M. Grove

Typeset in Cambria
Printed and bound in USA
Distributed in USA by Ingram,
Distributed in Canada by Hidden Brook Distribution
See BookManager – http://bookmanager.com/tbm/

Library and Archives Canada Cataloguing in Publication

Beatleman, Mark, author
        Living in the shadow : the skeleton of a pedophile found
lurking in the family closet / Mark Beatleman.

ISBN 978-1-927725-35-1 (paperback)

        1. Autobiographical fiction. I. Title.

PS8563.R75L58 2016   C813'.54   C2016-903890-4

Table of Contents

Acknowledgement

I would like to thank Hidden Brook Press for taking the risk in publishing my autobiographical story. Because I live in the USA it was natural for me to have sent my manuscript out to American publishers, small and large, but received nothing but rejections. Finally an agent was able to find a favorable response for my manuscript with Hidden Brook Press, a Canadian publisher. Their acquisitions editor, thank you Barbara Kelly, took a risk and passed it up the ladder to the publisher, who finally saw value in publishing, *Living in the Shadow*. After months of editing, they brought my manuscript to light. I thank Hidden Brook Press for their interest and courage in letting me tell my story.

Mark Beatleman

I would like to dedicate this book to those carrying a hook-clawed, fire-breathing dragon on their back as I have been for all of my adult life. Find the strength to loosen its grip on you and let it go as not being any part of the reborn you.

Mark Beatleman

Preface

I hope you read my preface. Because of the pedophile theme of this book and it being autobiographical, I hope that more people read this preface than might normally read a preface. I know that I have, typically, just skipped right into the first chapter of books and avoided any preambles. The first important issue for me was asking the question, can I still call this book autobiographical if I leave out some boring details and change some names? It would take you years to read my story if I included every detail of how I slipped down the slope to this point in time. Everything in this book is accurate and true though I have changed some names to protect individuals from scrutiny by the morbidly curious.

Flipping

Because this book is autobiographical I have received some criticism for flipping back and forth from first person to the third person narrator. It has been suggested that perhaps I have told portions in third person because of how close and painful some sections are for me. Maybe I needed to disassociate myself from telling the story. In the end I decided not to worry about the literary incongruities that might arise.

About Frank

Before I start my story I would like to thank my dear friend, Frank, for being part of my life. He knew nothing of my actions, with my daughter, in all of those years. It was not because of him being blind but it was because I was so skilled at hiding the truth about who I really was that he knew nothing. Basically, I compartmentalized my life. I would like to thank Frank from the bottom of my heart for sticking with me even after I finally confessed to him of my deeds. He was and still is a dear friend. He did not ever condone what I did; in fact he shared his disgust with me but never waved his finger at me. He trusted that those episodes of my life were truly well behind me by the time I confessed. I can only hope that others that have chosen to shun me will eventually forgive me and include me back into their lives, at least on some level.

The Purpose

I have mulled over just what is the purpose of writing an auto-biographical account of this portion of my life. In the beginning my therapist suggested that I write some notes in hopes that this process would open the door to me being honest with myself. He suggested that I could share the notes in our sessions, or not, it was totally up to me. For the most part I did not share the notes with him but I did find the process to be cathartic and well worth my while in articulating some of my thinking. For the most part I am not a writer. I have never shared even any small bits that I have written, even with Frank, Harrison or my ex-wives.

Years after I wrote my notes I found them in a computer

file and thought that I might write this book so that others confronted by their own claw-footed dragon might see that there is light at the end of their very long tunnel. I am now in my fifties. It took me years to even understand that I was in pain for what I had done. It took years for me to unhook the fire-breathing dragon from my back. It took even more years for the claw marks to finally heal over and stop bleeding. It took many painful years.

I contemplated suicide a number of times but in the end saw that there was a way that I could come to terms with what I had done. Some might say that I still have a long way to go but what can I say? The road that I am still on has been long, and full of potholes. I have discovered one important thing, and that is that life is the journey and you will never arrive at a full understanding of who you are. I now take more time on the journey to make sure that I do not hurt anyone as I move along the path. I spend more time looking at the consequences of my actions than I have ever done in the past.

Brother Harrison

I have decided to include a few letters and emails that were sent to me, over years, from my brother Harrison. Because of my collector, hording nature I had simply filed them away. They were at my fingertips when I started to write. In his emails to me he included a couple of emails to and from his friend Michael. At the time of receiving those emails from Harrison, I was perplexed and beyond annoyed that he had told anyone what I had done. I had been living in my own shadow for a long time and I was perplexed as to why he then sent them to me. I can only trust that it was important to Harrison that he had a friend to share this with and equally important that he let me know that he shared my story. The emails have been edited slightly to make them clearly pertinent to this book.

I included, in my story, a poem written by my brother Harrison so many years ago when I was an innocent child. I hope you see that once, I was a guiltless little boy. I look forward to being fully reborn and becoming the innocent boy that my big brother Harrison captured in his poem. I hope that Harrison does not mind me including his poem in this book. He has still not yet spoken to me after learning of my so-called depraved indiscretions with my daughter. As for my brother Jimmy he has never contacted me and I have little to say about him. His perspective does not fit much into my story.

Telling My Story

As I sat down to write this memoir I grappled with how to tell my story or even where to start – "I was born on a sunny, Monday, afternoon in 1955, in Gary Indiana…". – I know that was not the right place to start. I hope I don't jump in at a crazy place or jump around too much or leave anything important out.

The last thing I want to do with this story is to make excuses for my own darkness, my own so-called depravity. Have I actually learned to release this inner darkness, to let it go, or have I simply driven it deeper and deeper away from the surface of my life, my own consciousness, just so I can live with myself? My one hope is that if I have driven the darkness deep enough it might at least shrink and shrivel and vanish like something seen from a great distance, something that might die as it implodes and may finally be gone.

As I contemplate my story I have to wonder, which is the truth about me or in fact any individual, the dark or the light? How do I tell this story so that every reader is confronted by their own immorality, or at one end of the spectrum, by their own simple acts of unkindness? How do I tell my story so that every reader looks beyond their own persona of perfection, the persona that they let the public, let their family and friends see? I wonder, how does anyone reconcile that they are both, to a lesser or greater degree, the dark and the light; the dark and the light living compartmentalized, hidden one from the other?

Even after all of my wrestling with my conscience I still wonder how ashamed I am of my actions. Even though I am, without a doubt, the skeleton in my family closet, I still wonder if I am I simply the product of society or biology. As I grapple with my shame and as you read my story, you might wonder, are you the skeleton lurking in your family closet?

Mark Beatleman

Café Chat –
The Necessity of Change

A thin breeze filters through yellowing October. Dry leaves chatter their way across the patio into the corner. Mark Beatleman and his good friend Frank sit in the only sunny corner of the almost deserted patio bar. The whir of busy downtown traffic forced them to raise their voices from time to time.

"Frank, it is no wonder I am depressed, you're always nattering at me like some old hen about how I've gotta change my life and that I think too much about women and sex and need to find someone to love and settle down with. Don't bug me and tell me that I'm trapped in my little life of solitude and have to get out more. If I had a mother or a wife nattering at me I would say that I am being henpecked. Everyone, including you – everyone – is trapped in their own little lives and besides I'm quite happy with who I am and where I'm at. As far as sex goes, you are just jealous because I have more great sex in a weekend than you do in six months."

Mark's face flushes after raising his voice above the traffic, which dropped off to silence. He quickly lowers his pitch after he realized everyone was looking at him. Leaning forward he pushes his face closer to Frank.

In an almost whisper Mark hissed, "Everyone eventually stops fighting the inevitable barriers that hold them back that makes them feel trapped. Even my stupid, little, goldfish stopped fighting the impermeable barriers of a glass wall. Sometimes I feel like the stupid thing is smarter than I am. He quickly stopped bumping into the walls of his aquarium and resigned himself to the box life of being fed and gawked at."

A cool gray crawled up Mark's back. The late afternoon had crept up and over his shoulder. He shuffled his chair a bit to the left, now more in the sun he continued, "All my life I've felt like I was a goldfish trapped in a gurgling aquarium. A long time ago I learned not to bump into my glass prison walls as I peered out into the expanse of my limited universe, but nonetheless the barriers and limitations of life were there. I've always felt trapped in what seemed like an ever-shrinking aquarium. Me peering out, everyone else peering in, judging me, tapping on my glass wall asking why I did this or that, wanting me to jump out of the water and land in their lap of condemnation. Frank, don't you ever get depressed with life and wonder why you bother sticking around? I have to admit to myself that as I shrank into myself everyone simply left me alone in my little coffin size cubicle. Sure, sure, I know it is my own little, private, safe aquarium all of my own making. But it means I don't have to answer to anyone, not even myself if I don't want to. I figure that as long as my inbox is cleared by the end of the day my tiny-minded boss is happy. If he is happy then I am happy. Isn't that enough?

Mark stares for a few seconds at his drink on the table, as if still trying to fathom it all, then says "I know you have read 'Brave New World' by Huxley. Sometimes I wish I had a 'Soma' quota at the end of the workday to carry me until the morning alarm and maybe another to get me through the day. Heck I've wondered what it would be like to go on a nice long soma holiday and just never wake up. You wouldn't even know that you had died. First I would fuck my brains out with Ingrid. She was a good lay as long as we were nowhere that her husband would find us. We would take our last soma tab and just never wake up. That would do me just fine."

Reaching for his double shot of Scotch on the rocks he swigged his glass empty and plunked it down hard on the table. Mark shrugged and picked at a small hole in the tablecloth and then continued. "I don't know, maybe you're right. Maybe, I should get out more. I don't know what happened. Lately I've been peering out wondering what I am missing. Jim and Mary are heading to Jamaica for a holiday in February. You and Dorothy just got back from England and here I am, year after year, just making sure my in-box is clear by the end of the day. It's been going on like this for too long and I wonder why I am addicted to old episodes of "Friends". Maybe we all have to get out of our little aquariums sooner or later, I don't know. I'm too depressed to even think about it most of the time, let alone do anything about it." Mark shifted his chair further to the left again and rambled on.

"It's like the sun. Some people chase the sun, some people are chased by the shade, but some people are fortunate enough that no matter where they are, the sun will creep over the dark horizon and lay across their lap. What the hell am I doing wrong?"

More traffic rumbled by. Instead of raising his voice to compete, Mark just shut up and settled back into his seat. The shadows of the afternoon slowly, inevitably, crawled up the side of the checkered tablecloth and across the table. Neither Mark nor Frank spoke for the longest time. A thin cold breeze shivered them to pay their tab and move on.

*A Poem by my brother,
Harrison Beatleman*

A Journey Into the Dark

My little brother Mark
held my hand firm
in the now cool evening
of September.
"Don't be a sissy boy." I said.
"Mark, come with me.
Let me show you the stars."

We walked away
from the bright lights
of the front porch
into the dark
toward the open sky.
Silver stripes of dew painted
our naked legs as we walked
through the uncut grass
at the edge of the lawn
down into the distant hay field
north past the lane.

This was territory little Mark
had not yet ventured into
during the day
let alone at night.
I was the brave 13-year-old big brother,
Mark was 9 years younger
clinging close to my side
into the dark to see the brilliant sky
in a way that his tender innocence
had not yet been revealed to him.

Believe it or not I was once a tender innocent little boy, loved. One might say that I stole that innocence from my daughter, how tragic. I would say that her innocence and gaining it back is up to her and you. Is innocence in the eye of the beholder or is it a quality that can be lost forever.

Therapy Excerpt –
Beige

"I wish I knew how normal I am but that is for you to say, not me. Some describe me as being a self-confessed, paranoid, germaphobe, and Frank thinks that I have a dry, colorless imagination. This pretty much sums me up. How normal is all of this, I've no idea. I guess my mother and three ex-wives would describe me as beige. My mother constantly complained about the clothes I wore even as far back as when I was a young boy. No matter how she tried to jazz up my color choices I still gravitated to the same beige and gray choices that weaseled their way into my closet. My mother always tried her best to work me out of my drab persona by presenting a colorful cardigan for Christmas, a red shirt for my birthday but nothing seemed to make an impact. 'Different shades of gray and beige don't count as color choices,' she said time and time again.

"Many years later, after my mom died, my ex-wife, Mary, a flamboyant redhead that loved color, berated me with a daily mantra reminding me that beige was not only the color of my wardrobe, and apartment, but even more, my entire personality. Needless to say, that marriage lasted all of five minutes. Despite the hurtful rejection, I longed for her and offered to change. I was a sorry mess when she left me. I pleaded with her and showed up at her door wearing gray flannel pants and a beige shirt with a darker beige stripe incorporated into what I thought was a risqué loud pattern of disturbance. I loved her, I was committed and I wanted to show her I was willing to change for her; for the sake of our marriage, for our future children I was willing to wear any colors she wanted me to wear.

"It was at that time that I discovered the utter futility in trying to change my personality. You can change a leopard's spots but he is still a leopard. It is the deep down core of a person that makes them this way or that and I was, whether I liked it or not, Beige.

"I read something one time that said, 'Analyze your dreams and you will see the true color of your soul.' I discovered that I also dreamt in beige rather than in black and white like most so-called, normal people. It was my delight when I stepped out of the beige persona, even if only, subconsciously in a dream.

"Let me read you an email that I sent to Frank after a dream I had."

Email Subject Heading:
i dreamt in color last night

frank, u'll never guess what but i hd a dream in color last night. i can't remember when, if ever, i dreamed in color maybe never. everything is always in beige; sky, trees, grass, me and my clothes all in beige but this dream was in color, everything was in color. it was amazing. the trees were bright green ad the sky was a color of blue that i had never seen before but the funny thing is that it was night and all of the buildings were gray and the streets were gray but i was walking down the street, down the middle, there were no cars or anything anywhere but then when i got to the intersection i was standing waiting and waiting for the light to turn green. It stayed this brilliant red for the longest time and finally when i decided to cross the street against the red light there were four girls, maybe half of my age, pretty and they all had long beige hair, kind of like you see in movies but not as golden more beige than blond and as i was about to cross the street, even though the light was still red, one of the girls yells out, 'there is one don't let him get away' and they started to run towards me so i started to run away and eventually they caught up to me even though i was running as fast as i could they threw me down in the middle of the street and started to make love to me in a vicious kind of way and not one at a time man but all at the same time. i was naked and they were naked and their breasts rubbed all over me and their beige hair was dangling in my face as we made love. we were just one big ball of intertwined beige bodies embroiled in a steamy ultimate release and then eventually i lay there ex-hausted and the girls were gone and everything turned back to black and white. AND THEN I WOKE UP!!!!!!!!!!!!!!!!! and i had to pee real bad but i couldn't until the swelling went down and then I just sat on the side of my bed and laughed and laughed. i don't know if my neighbors could hear me laughing at three in the morning or not but i just laughed and laughed. Man i needed that laugh.

btw give me a call and let me know how your trip went.

ttys mark

"After I clicked send I wondered what Sigmund Freud would say about that dream. I don't know if I ever told you but I took a psych 101 class back in my university days. I started wondering what it all meant. What on earth does beige hair mean? Was I aroused by the beige banality of my own sexuality? The abandoned intersection, traveling from nowhere, to nowhere, arriving nowhere, ravaged by the unattainable yet ultimately abandoned, waking to the reality of disappointment, waking to aloneness, raped, used – even if momentarily willing, even if encouraging. Why were the girls only half my age? That made them pretty young teenagers? If Freud was right then I was not just the ravaged but the ravager. I was not just myself or even just the girls but it was also the streets, empty. I was the long stoplight that never turned green, I was the lost, desolate city, gray. And then as I pondered the hidden psychological meanings my chuckles of delight turned to despair.

"Well, by then I was wide awake and in no mood to go back to sleep so I slipped on a pair of my old tattered moccasin slippers that I had mended with silver duct tape. It was a nice night but I was hit by the chilly air as I stepped off the back deck into the dark night. The dew covered everything. Stars filled the sky like I had never seen before. I walked out to the quiet streets of Gary, Indiana and meandered aimlessly in the direction of flashing neon. It was really quiet, almost dead. I nodded to Mario flipping some pizza dough in the window of 'Mama Gino's'. I wandered past the wine store, past the Good Will secondhand store where most of my drab wardrobe was carefully selected.

"I stopped in front of 'Nickie's Second-Hand Wonders' and wondered if they had ever sold an LP from their twenty-five cent sale bin. It is funny but I stared at myself in the window. All of a sudden there were no cars, no bikes, no traffic noise of any kind. I smirked; I was in the abandoned city of my nightmare looking past my beige shirt to the dull gray of privation. I flinched back into reality as the traffic light turned green bringing the sounds of the city gently back to life; traffic droned, silencing the clinking of my generosity, coins tossed into the hat of a street person, slumped; snoring echoed in the hollow door well. Without stopping, I ambled home exhausted, hoping I could return to sleep.

Mark slumped back in his chair. "Sorry I rambled on a bit and I know we are just about out of time but what do you think of my dream? And don't you dare just turn it back on me and ask what I think. I already told you what I think. I want to know what you think."

Therapy Excerpt –
Private Space

"I don't know why. I just hate the Gary Indiana Transit System. I don't know why. It is just one of my least favorite places to spend time. Not only don't I like where it is taking me every morning but I vehemently disliked the jammed proximity of sharing space and air with anyone, let alone total strangers. It's crazy to say but even with all three of my ex-wives they eventually took up too much of what I call 'my' private space. I don't know why but I never learned how to comfortably share a bed or even a sofa, let alone air space with any of them. Soon after each marriage began I grew less and less tolerant of what I called 'obligatory snuggle time' even while watching TV. I don't think that I realized it for years but the only good reason for snuggle time, for me, was simply because it was a prelude to sex. An axiom of life that I've always advocated is that women liked to snuggle and men liked to have sex. Men tolerated snuggle time only for the reward of sex. You're a guy. What do you think? Some women tolerate sex just to get a few minutes of snuggle time. I guess one had better choose your sex or snuggle partner carefully.

"I know that you aren't going to tell me what you think so let's leave it as a rhetorical question. The fact is I even resented sharing the bathroom sink while brushing my teeth and I most certainly would never, under any circumstance, share a toothbrush, let alone a mint, or let my wife take a lick from my ice cream cone. I've read enough psychobabble stuff in Psych 101 to know what you're going to say, I can even see you writing it down as I speak. "His tolerance for sharing intimacies is nil. He is afraid of not being loved. Giving up anything, even an inch on the sofa really represented his fear of rejection and a desire to maintain distance and control in fear of being rejected – or something like that. Am I close? Who cares? It is all just a bunch of psychobabble anyway. I sometimes wonder why I even come once a week to see you.

"If I was so afraid of commitment and such an unloving person you might wonder how it is that I ended up living with and taking care of my two daughters as a single father but you never asked me anything about that. What is it you want to talk about today? Forget about it. Let me tell you about my crazy wives. One was a schizophrenic, manic-depressive; and one was an alcoholic, a total lush and had a secret life as a stripper and hooker that she kept from me even when we were married; and one was just downright a crazy and controlling bitch that didn't give me a moment's peace of mind just to relax and watch TV before I did the dishes or took out the garbage. She browbeat me about leaving the toilet seat up or how I squeezed the toothpaste in the middle or if I left a bit of toothpaste in the sink. She bitched about me leaving my dirty socks at the end of the bed even if I picked them up in the morning. One time she flipped out, yelling at me because I put her toothbrush on the back of the toilet because that is not where you put a toothbrush that has to go in your mouth. She didn't want to know that I picked it up off of the floor for her, from behind the toilet, she just threw it in the garbage. I was waiting for her to stick it in her mouth. I would have choked on my laughter if she had done that. Instead of letting her nag me to death I put a few of my things in a bag and just walked out. I even remember the day. She was nagging at me about something and I just walked out without saying a word. I never went back. I never even went back for any of my stuff.

"Yah – both of my daughters came from my first wife. One week she was up and cheerful and loved cooking and cleaning and even loved sex but then the next week she was a slovenly bitch and accused me of raping her and called the police. She was just nuts. One week she would get a great job and the next week she would lose it because she couldn't get out of bed to go to work. I tried to live with it for years but eventually she scared the girls one too many times. Up, down, up, down, up, down. It finally drove me and my daughters nuts so when I finally left her I took the girls and moved into a little one-bedroom apartment. When a judge finally gave me custody of the girls I got a bigger place and took care of them as a single dad. They were about four and six at the time and moved out only when they went off to college. It was an ok life at the time. I was on welfare and did just about everything for my girls. Rose got to see the girls every other weekend. Sometimes the girls and I would go to visit their grandmother - Nanna Dorie – is what they called her. She was an ok grandmother. She even helped me get custody of the girls because she knew how wacko Rose was. Now, of course, she hates my guts for what I did to Rachel. She said she would cut off my nuts if she ever saw me again. Never mind what a good father I was for all of those years."

Therapy Excerpt – Wheelbarrows Full of Horseshit

"It seems every time I turn around I have another nightmare to tell you. I didn't used to have nightmares. It was such an awful night. I sat up and swung my legs to the side of the bed and felt disoriented for the longest time. My shoulders were heavy and aching as I slumped my elbows to my knees and rubbed my eyes over and over again. It was dark and all I could see was the red haze that radiated from the bedside clock beaming 3:54 am. The last few minutes, or had it been hours, seemed so close to the truth of my life that I was disoriented. The confusion of this being a nightmare or memory fumbled in my brain as I struggled to consciousness.

"Why had Harrison been on the road with me? But there he was, clear as day, walking two paces in front of me. How on earth did I get stuck walking home behind him. My brother, who refuses to speak to me. I haven't even seen him in who knows how long. I haven't even spoken to him for years ever since he and the family found out about me having sex with Rachel." Mark involuntarily rubbed his eyes, pulled a piece of paper out of his pocket started to read as if it were a story he found in a magazine.

Without turning to Mark, his brother pivoted in his tracks, slipped on a pair of pristine, white satin gloves, picked up the handles of his wheelbarrow and started, at a quick pace, to walk towards home. After a moment of hesitation Mark grabbed his white satin gloves, grasped the handles of his own wheelbarrow and hurried off to catch up.

Despite the fact that Harrison had disowned Mark years ago, here was Mark trotting down the gravel road trying to catch up to him, both of them pushing wheelbarrows full of fresh, stinking horseshit. Still a few paces behind his brother, Mark wondered what the hell he was supposed to do? Break out into song, give him a cheery back smacking – "So how you doing bro?" He felt like saying "Hey you bastard, if I have to push this load of horseshit with you, you ARE going to tell me how you got in my dream and how you got to be such a sullen son-of-a-bitch with me. What the hell did I ever do to you to warrant pushing a wheelbarrow full of horse crap downwind from you?"

A smirk came over Mark's face with a subtle strategy. He would let his pace slow, bit by bit. He would pull back and let more and more distance fall between them. He would play a game to see if his brother would even notice. The palpable quiet was interrupted only by the rhythmical squeaking of their wheelbarrows timed with the drumming of footfalls.

The greater the distance, the greater the relief of not having to share space with his brother, but still the stink of his own horseshit filled his path. With consternation, Mark mumbled to himself, "I have, for too many years, shared my life with him; I don't need to share another, single breath and smell the horseshit he is pushing around."

With every step, Mark wondered what was going through his brother's mind. His brother's normal aloof demeanor, his speechlessness is well rehearsed with years of silence under his belt. Whatever was going through his mind he walked in stoic silence, in an unvaried quick pace. Mark said out loud to himself, "Thank God, I am finally alone." His pace lessened until he could finally slip, out of sight, behind a tree. Even if his brother were to turn now Mark would have vanished, he would not even be a footprint in the dust behind him. He would not be the squeak of a wheel or the shuffle of shoes on gravel. He simply would not be.

From Mark's vantage point his brother does not turn to look where he is. His pace does not deviate. Mark mumbles out loud to himself. "Is he deaf? Did he forget that I was there? Does he have no imagination whatsoever? Maybe I fell behind him and was dying in the dust." Maybe that would not matter to his brother. Never did he turn, not even once to see or say anything. His steady pace was unwavering, unyielding.

Mark sat in the shade on the rim of his stinking wheelbarrow behind the tree. No brother in sight, sheltered from the penetrating sun he felt a sad, dry breeze blow the aroma of manure across the empty field. The stench of his own wheelbarrow was all-pervasive. Mark reached over and flicked off the night light. Rubbed his eyes and slumped back into bed. He pressed his head into his still hot pillow. There would be little sleep for him that night.

Mark slumped in the big wing-back chair and crossed his arms. "So there you go. That is my, pushing a wheelbarrow full of horseshit, story. I don't even want to know what you think of it. It is pretty obvious that I've been pushing my own stinkin' load of shit around while I try to make it back home and I think my brother has his own load of shit to deal with but he doesn't want to talk to me about it. All it makes me is tired."

Therapy Excerpt –
The Other Skeleton in the Closet

"Why do we always have to get back to Rachel and Selene? What is so important about my relationship with my daughters? Why is my relationship with them more important than my relationship with my brother Harrison who hates me and won't talk to me? Last week I told you about my brother and my dream about pushing a load of horseshit around in a wheelbarrow and now you just want to swing straight into talking about my daughters again. Don't you know enough about them yet?

"Before I tell you more about Rachel and Selene I want to tell you something more about Harrison that I didn't tell you about last week because we ran out of time. It is more about the dream and him and me pushing the wheelbarrows full of horseshit. Well what I didn't tell you is that Harrison molested his daughter and went to jail. Yah that's real life shit, not part of the dream. That is the shit that he has been carrying around with him. That is why he doesn't want to talk to me now in real life and why he didn't want to talk to me in the dream while he was pushing his wheelbarrow full of horseshit, both of us with our lily white gloves on, noses in the air. There we were walking into the aroma of our own horseshit. Every step we took it was inevitable that we would be walking in the smell of our own shit and I was trying to keep up with him and he was ignoring me then I finally just let him go on without me.

"He doesn't want to talk with me in real life because he knows that he and I are too much alike. The fact is that he just got off of the slippery slope and didn't have sex with his daughter. Basically what he did was touch his daughter's nipples. Society says he molested her. I think he said twice, while he thought that she was asleep and then right after each time he put her hand on his penis. Both times while he thought that she was asleep. At least that is what he told me and I guess I believe him. He said he was so freaked out at what he did he never did it again and signed up with a shrink. Then he went to jail for three weeks because it turns out she wasn't asleep and his daughter told her mom, his ex-wife, and she told a teacher and the teacher told the police. I think that the conviction was for sexual exploitation or something like that. He swore it never happened again and I believe him but now he is all high and mighty with me and he thinks that he is better than me because he didn't rape his daughter. He so called, "just" touched her while he thought she was asleep. The fucker calls me a pedophile and he was just the same as me and now he is pushing the same wheelbarrow of horseshit as me. What I think is that the law said he molested his daughter and that is different than what happened between me and my daughter. We made love for years and it wasn't rape.

"Yah I know you want me to get back to Rachel but I just had to tell you what really happened and what my dream was all about. With Rachel I don't remember how it started. Rachel wanted it and I wanted it and it just happened. She was horny and I was horny. What more does it take? It wasn't rape, we made love every time. It's not like I tied her up, beat her, threw her on the floor and fucked her up the ass like some moron hillbilly. I didn't rape her if that is what you're trying to get me to say. It was actually kind of tender and nice. I know society thinks that I raped her but actually I think that it is our limiting, constricted, anxiety-driven society that is fucked-up, not me.

"The first time we actually made love wasn't for quite a while after we both wanted it. It all happened because of the shower. Yah, the shower. One time I was in the shower with her washing her hair like we always did and she slipped or something and grabbed on to me around my waist so she wouldn't fall. Hot water was streaming over both of us, steam filled the room and I was suddenly overcome by how soft and sexy she was. I had never thought of her that way before. I really mean it. I never did. I started to wash her back while she was pressed up against me and I rubbed soap over her and up over her shoulders and she just stood there and let me wash her and I washed up her legs and between her legs and I washed her vagina and I put my finger partly inside her but she slightly winced with pain so I stopped. That was the first time that anything sex-like happened and that is all that happened. I got a hard-on but I tried to hide it from her. We got out of the shower and I wrapped her in a big towel, dried her hair and sent her off to get her and her sister dressed so we could all leave. That was when she was about twelve or so. I don't remember exactly.

"What do you mean what happened then? I just told

you. Nothing. No, I didn't just leave then. Well yah. After she left and I locked the bathroom door I jerked off. I had a hard on. What of it. I jerked off, I shaved, I got dressed and we went out to meet their mother and grandma for dinner like we always did on a Sunday afternoon. The girls want to see their mom so I take them. I can't stand my fuckin' ex but I gotta take them and be as nice as pie to her. Delores is the girls' grandmother, they call her Nanna Dorie. She keeps saying to just be nice, be nice for the sake of the girls. It's all one big f-in' lie but I do it anyway. I lie so much about my f-in' ex-wife that I start thinking that I might actually like her and we should get back together again and then she opens her mouth and says some bone-head thing and calls me lazy in front of my girls and all I want to do is smack her but I never do. I was taught never to be violent to a girl. Everyone thinks that I am the lazy, stay-at-home dad sucking money from her wallet but nobody has any idea what I gotta put up with.

"Yah, ok back to Rachel. People think that I must have been raping her and just fuckin' her like you see on some violent TV cop show but that isn't what happened at all. I love Rachel, I love both my daughters. A few days later I gave both girls a shower again but I got out first because it was too crowded in there for three people. The girls like having a shower together so I just left them to play and get washed and yah before you ask, I jerked off in the bedroom while they were in the shower so they wouldn't catch me. I don't know why I had a hard-on but I just did and I jerked off.

"I don't know how many times I showered with them after that time but every time I had a shower just with Rachel I washed her hair and she put her arms around like she did the first time when she slipped. From then on I washed her hair and then her back and then I never stopped and she always liked it. She always let me wash her vagina. It used to turn her on. Yah, I put my finger in her all the way after a few times. She winced in the beginning but I knew she liked it because she never stopped me. She never even tried to stop me. She just opened her legs. It was like an invitation. I don't know how many times we had sex. It was maybe once a week for about six years. Sometimes twice a week. Sometimes once a month but it was never just sex, it was making love every time."

Café Chat –

Raccoon Trappin'

Mark and Frank sat in their favorite coffee shop, each leaning over a low-fat double cappuccino. Mark was boasting about his latest sex conquests and how young and pretty she was. He put down his New Yorker and leaned towards Frank. "No this is a new chick, June or May or something like that. I can't remember the names of the ones that aren't keepers. You're thinking of Ingrid. I told you about Ingrid, the sexy motorcycle chick but anyway she and I split up a couple of weeks ago. Man, she was so hot. I must have told you about her and that we split up. I told you that Ingrid dumped me for her husband? I can't believe it. For months she has been talking about leaving him, getting a divorce and marrying me. I was crushed for days. I can't believe it. She can't tell me that sex was better with him than with me. She was awesome in the sack. Do you know how many of her footprints are on the ceiling of my van? Heck, I'm still crushed.

"The husband was such a dweeb. I couldn't stand him. I met him a few times at parties and BBQs. She could have been fucking me right under his nose and I swear he wouldn't notice. He had his nose buried too deep in his guns. He was a gunsmith and collector or something like that. That kind of made me nervous so maybe it is just as well that she went back to him. I was going to buy his Harley from him but I couldn't come up with the bread. Ingrid and I were going to ride together. She had a bright red Harley, a bit smaller than his. She looked so sexy in her black leathers.

"My girls even liked her. She treated them real well but I don't see my girls much these days since Rachel moved south to Indianapolis. From Gary to the Nap is just too far to go. I can hardly keep up the payments on the van let alone the extra gas.

"Frank, I've got a raccoon living at my place. Damn thing keeps digging in my compost dragging sloppy stuff around making a mess. She's living in my lawnmower shed. Damn thing. Scares the crap out of me at night every time I go in the back yard. She sits there in the dark where I can't see her. Then all of a sudden she moves, she hisses at me and dashes off because I get too close. Gets my heart jumping every time. Damn thing.

"I guess you wouldn't happen to have a live coon trap I can borrow? I gotta get rid of the beggar but I don't want to kill her. If I don't get rid of her she'll have babies in the spring and then I'll have a family of trouble to get rid of. That's all I need is a bunch of black-eyed bandits raiding my compost pile and digging in my little garden.

"I might have to drive out to my uncle's place and see if he still has one I can borrow. He trapped one once. He used sardines as bait — caught a cat. Cat looked like a raccoon in the dark so he left it in the trap all night and called Animal Control the next morning. It wasn't until they arrived that my uncle felt damn silly. Turned out it was the neighbor's cat. He never liked the damn thing. Even though it stayed away after that, he figured it was a waste of good sardines.

"My neighbor said he used to have a live raccoon trap but he threw it in the lake — raccoon was still in it. Poor beggar. I gotta get rid of my raccoon. It's driving me crazy, damn thing. I think I'll trap it and take it over to Ingrid's place and chuck it in her pool or kill it and hang it on her Harley. I'm just kidding. I wouldn't kill it. Everything deserves to live I figure. I don't know how some people can be so cruel."

Therapy Excerpt –
A Good Girl She Was

"You want me to talk about Rachel again? I can if you like but I don't see the point. She was just a normal girl. There isn't much to say. She did just ok in school but she was way brighter than she let on to anyone. She just plugged along and didn't do much that was remarkable or brilliant but she was a good girl and didn't give anyone any trouble about anything. If you told her to finish her dinner, she finished her dinner. If you told her to go to bed in ten minutes, she went to bed in nine. She didn't argue with anyone about anything like her little sister, Selene, used to. Oh man she was the scrapper in the family.

"When all of this started Rachel was twelve. She was tall for a twelve-year-old and just starting to get boobs. The top of her head came to about just under my chin. I remember because her face pressed up against my chest when she gave me a hug. She would almost coo like a dove when I hugged her back. The one thing that she had going for her was that she was real pretty and she knew it. Her mother gave her a girl's make-up kit with blush and eye stuff and a lip gloss for her birthday when she turned thirteen. Right after she unwrapped it she took it into the bathroom, locked the door and came out twenty minutes later looking like a painted hooker. She looked about ten years older and everyone at the party said how pretty she looked and how grown up she looked. Her grandma Dorie even showed her how to do up her eyes better so she didn't look so much like a slut. I hated that stuff on her face. As far as I was concerned she was way too young for makeup.

"She never did understand why I didn't like her to wear the makeup when we went to visit my mom and dad. I just knew that they would not approve, but I thought she just looked pretty without any gunk on her face. One time when she was about fourteen or maybe a bit older my dad saw her wearing lots of makeup and made some comment about her being gussied up and looking like a tramp. She never wore makeup to their house again.

"Yah my youngest daughter, Selene, was the smart one and didn't care too much for makeup. It's not that she was a gay or anything, it's just that maybe her sister wore enough makeup for the two of them.

Boys? Rachel? Yah she always had lots of boys hangin' around her at school even when she was twelve. I always had to keep an eye on her when she had friends over after school. I didn't want any hanky-panky going on behind my back. I know what kids can get up to when you aren't lookin'. I didn't want my girls to end up pregnant like my ex-wife did before we got married. My first wife and I got married in a rush so the bun in the oven wouldn't show at the wedding.

"What do you mean by do I realize what I just said?"

It's All Just
a Bunch of Psychobabble

The wall heater thundered to life. Hot air courses into the room. A gray ceiling fan hangs motionless over Mark's bed collecting dust. Morning light slivers in through closed drapes. Mark reluctantly creeps into consciousness.

Leaning forward over the bathroom sink, Mark, pushes his anemic face towards the steamed mirror and rubs his hands over his morning stubble. He pulls down on his cheeks looking past his tired complexion into bulging red eyes. He is oblivious to his hand-written note that is stuck to the mirror. "Think Positive. You Will Make It. It's Only a Matter of Persistence." The note is curled, faded, spotted; God only knows how long it has been ignored morning after morning.

In a low grumbling voice Mark pokes at his teeth and mumbles, "We're all afraid of something." Toweling steam from the mirror he sticks his tongue out as far as it will go, looks down to his tonsils and rubs his neck. He squints his eyes and continues with his habitual manner of talking to himself. He says with whining cynicism, "My shrink says I'm afraid of finding out what I am afraid of. Supposedly I'm afraid of finding out just what's holding me back from making a real commitment to any woman. It might cause change and change can be painful he says. Fear of the unknown. Hell, it all sounds like psychobabble to me."

Mark rolls his eyes and thinks to himself. "Mark Beatleman you are pluggin' along nickel by nickel, worrying about every penny, wondering what you did to deserve this so-called sorry life that you live." He rocks his shoulders back and forth and rubs his face again. "I have three failed marriages under my belt; Rose, Mary and Ruth. My shrink says that I'm still clinging to my second ex-wife so much that I can't move more than two blocks away from her. Damn, I spent my last penny to buy Mary a lawnmower but then what did I bloody well do for fuck sakes? I also cut her grass. Why the hell I didn't just give it to her 17-year-old kid to push is beyond me?" Mark thumps the side of his head with the heel of his hand and rolls his eyes at the mirror.

With quick, agitated strokes, Mark slashes at his beard with his new, car-sleek, red Schick razor, guaranteed-to-make-any-women-want-to-kiss-his-baby-smooth face. "My shrink says I was looking for – 'come back to me pity points'. More psychobabble if you ask me. Can't we just do something good without it having a hidden agenda? Next time I won't tell him if I do something kind and generous for my ex. I'll just tell him when I do something spiteful and mean. Next week I'll just make something up and see what he has to say about that. I'll tell him that I do good things for people because I am compensating for having had sex with my daughter. That'll make his wheels spin. He'll think I'm making progress and he will be delighted."

Mark takes a step back from the sink. Still only half-shaven he points at the mirror. "It's my job, that's what keeps me here, not my ex-wives and it isn't Ingrid. She can go fuck herself. It's my job, nothin' but my job that keeps me here. That's why I stick around this place, not because I want to get back with my ex-wife. Besides, it wouldn't matter, she doesn't want me anyway. I can't see that changing even if I wanted it to, which I don't." Mark leans forward with hands on the cold white porcelain and looks himself straight in the eye. "Which I don't!" He mumbles to himself, "I'll move back to my hometown when I'm good and ready and not a minute sooner and meanwhile I'm damn proud of my job." He shrinks back down to a normal posture and almost whines. "I finally climbed two rungs up the ladder but I still always feel like I've got one foot on the ground stuck in the mud. Why is the damn ladder so damn slippery?"

Leaning back from the mirror Mark points back at his reflection again, "It's the system. That's what it is. You can't only have bosses; you have to have grunt workers at the bottom and lots of them and even plenty of them sitting on a shelf like canned peas waiting to be used. I used to be one of them cans of peas when I worked in the warehouse. Heck I still am one. I just got a raise and a bit of respect from my boss, but I'm still a ground level grunt worker wishing I could earn enough to buy a house instead of renting. What on earth am I doing wrong? All I want is a house, a garden, a car and a family to come home to after a long day of work. What I want is a wife. That's why Ingrid left me. Because I'm dirt poor and why the fuck would she leave a gorgeous house with a pool to move into a dump like this. My daughters moved hundreds of miles just to get away from me. What the fuck did I do wrong with my life?"

Bringing the towel to his face he sniffs at it, wrinkles his nose, sniffs again and tosses it into a growing pile beside the door. Slashing at his face Mark finishes shaving, splashes "Old Spice" on his face then into his arm pits and mumbles, "Before my brother found out about me and Rachel he wanted me to move back home. My brooottthhher wanted me to get half of the money out of my ex-wife's house. My brooottthhher wanted me to move to his little flea-bitten town, come over for dinner twice a week and live happily ever after. My brooottthhher wanted... what my brother wanted was for me to rent a truck and move. I can't afford to rent a damn truck, let alone start looking for a job in a totally different country. Besides that he won't even speak to me right now, so fuck that!" Mark reaches for the tossed towel and dries his face.

Mark slams down the handle on the toaster and resumes mumbling to himself as if Frank was standing beside him. "Afraid of success, my shrink said, or was that afraid of failure? I still don't understand the bloody difference. It's just more psychobabble to me. How about afraid of not paying my rent? I bounced my rent check last month because I was five bucks short. Now that's real – not psychobabble.

"Holy crap, look at the time. I had better get in gear. Maybe if I stopped going to the damn shrink I could afford to rent a truck and move. Maybe after I get a raise." Mark jots down a note on a scrap envelope pulled from the recycle box and places it on the table just before he slams the door behind him.

'Don't forget to take out Rose's garbage tonight.'

A Thread of Emails from Brother Harrison

Dear Mark, I still can't cope with talking to you. It has only been a few weeks since I found out that you had been raping your daughter for six years. My head is still spinning, I send you these two emails so you know how messed up I am about what you did even though it has been years since you stopped. You should know that just about everyone in the family, including friends, know what you did. There is a varying range of reactions but the general consensus is that you should just stay away, maybe for a long time.

I can't talk but I send my regards.

Harrison

Dear Michael

My head is spinning. I learned last week that my brother, Mark, had been raping his daughter, Rachel, for 6 years from when she was 12 to 18. She is now 25. It has sent my head spinning. How is this possible that someone you loved and respected could be so depraved and you didn't have a clue what was going on? It is like finding a skeleton in your closet. Your Uncle Harry has been missing for twenty years, murdered by your aunt Mable whom you have loved dearly for years and had lunch with you every Sunday after church and she has been telling you that Uncle Harry doesn't come to lunch because he is just not feeling well and now you wonder really what happened to your missing pet Rover and start thinking that maybe Aunt Mable did him in after he scratched her nylons years ago. Everything starts to sound absurd. I wish I could understand.

So how is that for a bombshell dropped on your day?

I hope to see you soon, I need to talk in person and see if I can make any sense of this.

All the best,
Harrison

Dear Harrison, You are right, that is a bombshell. My God, what a shock but it is maybe better than finding Uncle Harries skeleton in your closet. First I thought that maybe you were pulling my leg. Thank you for sharing this with me, a sign of the trust and love between us. That is horrible, very sad that someone could do such a thing, break the bond of trust between father and daughter. There is this animal nature in us that if we are weak it gains power and overcomes us. Most of us have demonistic thoughts in some way or another but we find ways to build fortifications to that beast. God helps in that, divine Love, we can't do it on our own. We have to turn to the divine somehow, even those who do not believe in a particular version of God. May he, one day, will be forgiven for his actions, on this side or the other side of the grave. Aside from his dear beloved daughter, he must also be suffering for what he has done. May he suffer in the name of redemption rather than suffer simply because of the fear of being caught. When our wrongdoings hurt others, especially those we love, we are hurt, every one of us. He must have his share of suffering. Think of his suffering and forgive dear friend, you do have that capacity.

Love, Michael

Therapy Excerpt –
Father was a bit of a Tough Cookie

"I have been wondering when you might want me to talk about my father. He was a bit of a tough cookie sometimes. One time he punched me in the face because I was aggravating him about something. I can't even remember what it was but it was only teenage crap. He almost broke my nose. He turned and looked me right in the face with his fist raised and said if I told mother he would punch me in the face twice next time. He would have done it too. I learned quick to keep my mouth shut. My older brothers, Harrison and Jim and I had all been molested by him and we all kept our mouths shut. Who knows what else he did and to who. I was too young to remember but Harrison said that our dad went to each of our beds and played with our penises a few times. Harrison said he just pretended that he was asleep and actually just laid there and enjoyed it. He said that he never told anyone until he told me a few years ago. Same with Jimmy. We never told anyone else as far as I can tell.

"Even though people thought that my dad was mostly a nice guy and a pillar in the church and a good salesman all his life, he could turn on a dime. At the very least he could easily be argumentative and pugnacious. I could tell you so many stories about how grumpy my father was one day and then play with us the next but I don't know why you want me to talk about my father. He doesn't have anything to do with me and Rachel. My relationship with my father was totally different from my relationship with Rachel and Selene. My relationship with my daughters was near perfect but we talked a lot, laughed and when they were growing up we did just about everything together. We didn't have much money, but that's ok. No matter what money you have or don't have, you can't have everything you want and you sure as heck don't get what you deserve, so sometimes you just gotta take what you think you deserve.

"Yah there were some good times. We used to go camping every summer for a couple of weeks. We never had a cottage but we had a trailer. On weekends we would go to my aunts' and uncles' cottages but for a longer holiday in the summer we went on road trips. My brothers and I were the ones who made the fire every day and went out looking for wood in the forest. That was the best part of the holiday. We would come back to the campsite with our arms loaded. Mom and dad didn't know that we would steal wood from other campsites when we could. It was a lot easier than dragging branches from the forest. I think that my dad knew but he never let on."

Therapy Excerpt –
The Fly Sucked Dry by the Spider

"Yah, of course I know what she was thinking. I know exactly what she was thinking. We actually talked about it. You think that I don't know what is going on in my own daughter's mind? You think that I don't know what is good or bad for her? It is society that has fucked her up not me. She said that she enjoyed making love with me. She liked it. Is that so hard to believe that she liked it? In fact she even sought it out and even got jealous if I looked at another woman. If I had a girlfriend, I mostly had to keep the two of them apart. She always hated my girlfriends and tried to split us up.

"The true shame, of so called incest, is that society does not condone it and does not see the love and beauty of it in some cases. The true shame is that the child or even the adult child sometimes can't just move on to a new relationship when it is time. Like all relationships, they come to an end and sometimes it is painful. Like most people, I've had a few painful split-ups in my life but we eventually get over them. Some are more painful than others. The sad thing for the so called abused person is moving on to another relationship, and that they always tell someone, and then like my daughter they are instantly caught in this disgusting web of shame that is inflicted on them that they can't get out of. The only way out for the child, even as a now adult, is to learn to hate the adult by calling it abuse. Instead they should just move on. But they can't because of the hideous web of hate that society has woven. They become the fly sucked dry by the spider. If they just kept it to themselves they could just move on to another relationship and not be fucked-up.

"Have you ever heard of Warren Farrell and what he said in his article in 1977 about the positive aspects of incest? Well basically, I can't remember exactly, but in an interview, he argued that incest could be a good thing for everyone involved. If I remember properly he said, that 'incest is like a magnifying glass and that in some circumstances it magnifies the beauty of the relationship, and in others it magnifies the trauma.' In an interview, he said, and I even remember it exactly '…but the inference is that all incest is abuse. And that's not true.' Between my daughter and me it was love and it magnified the beauty until society got involved and fucked it up and said it was wrong and dirty and called me a pedophile. I abhor that word. Pedophile. It implies such social disgust.

"'There is nothing good or bad, but thinking makes it so.' I can't remember who said that. Was it Shakespeare? Or I think it was Einstein? It doesn't matter because it is true. Incest is bad only because of what society says not because it truly is. My daughter, years after we moved on to other relationships and were fine with moving on and fine with our years of making love, and got along with each other just fine, eventually told her then boyfriend and he flipped out. Because he was a trained social worker, he convinced her that she was abused and fucked-up. I feel like I was thrown under the bus by my own daughter with her telling her boyfriend and by her believing what he had to say about our making love. He's one fucked-up individual. But I guess I can't blame him. He's just a product of society.

"I was reading stuff on the internet about incest and there was this girl that said she was raped by her father for years and she was intrigued by being able to do adult things like having sex and knowing things that other kids didn't know. She said she loved being wanted and loved and she loved being the favorite. She learned at an early age that she had power in her sexuality, even at the age of eleven. She said that she learned to be sexy at an early age and it gained her attention, and attention gained her power. I figure that she must have been a smart girl.

"I'm not trying to say that what I did to my daughter was right but this girl kind of suggests that there are more than one way for a girl to react after sex with an adult. She even says that the true shame of being abused as a child is that if you don't feel about it the way you 'should' feel about it, people think you're fucked-up. She said that people want to pity you and when you don't give them anything to pity, they say you're as sick as your molester."

Therapy Excerpt –
Pedophilia

"Pedophile, is such a dirty word. I hate anyone thinking that I was a pedophile. I even looked it up in Wikipedia. It said that a pedophile is a guy who has sex with a girl that is eleven or younger. Rachel was twelve when we had sex the first time and the fact is we didn't have sex, we made love. Sex is somehow a different emotionally charged word than 'making love'. We made love like adults. That makes me sick to think that someone would fuck a little kid. They should be shot for fuck sakes."

Letter 1 –

Dear Brother Mark

Dear Mark:

I have had a difficult past six months since learning of your moral infraction but I am sure it has been tenfold more difficult for you – at least I can only hope.

I have compassion and love for you, brother. While what you did was despicable, I am in the process of separating action from person and seeing your true spiritual likeness as a loving, caring individual. This has been difficult for me partly because of my own self-condemnation for things, thoughts, actions that I have committed in the past. You are a painful reminder of who I was, and who I could have been if I had taken another wrong turn and followed you down the same path. I condemn you because I condemn myself, brother. As you know, I was in therapy for a long time before and after my conviction of sexual exploitation and serving three weeks in jail. That therapy was of pivotal importance to my spiritual and emotional growth. I will push, no more, against your resistance that you need therapy. I hope you one day recognize the value of professional help for yourself even though you say you will never commit such an infraction ever again. I can understand your being so embarrassed that you would not even want to divulge your actions, even to a therapist stranger.

After I learned about your past sexual relationship with your daughter, I contacted a therapist and had two sessions to simply help me think through what it is you did and its impact on me, let alone the impact on our entire family and your daughters. He and I felt that these two sessions were all I needed. I have moved on without further assistance from him but my mind keeps flashing to years of you raping your daughter. I look forward to the day that I can look at you and not see a pedophile rapist.

You have probably received the package that I sent you with spiritual articles about 'the sexually abused and the sexual abuser'. I hope you will read them and find some spiritual growth through the contemplation of seeing beyond the abuser and the abused. Read them more than once, as I did. Write notes and study them as you apply the spiritual concepts to you and your daughter. I hope that we can, in the future, talk and grow back to something similar to what we had as brothers.

Part of my difficulty is going to be looking past the lie that you presented to me for all of those years while you raped your daughter. I am angry that you lied to me, brother. I am angry that you could not come to me and confess when you had just the thought of rape and incest. I understand the difficulty of confessing rape to me, but I thought that we were close enough that you could have confessed the "thought of rape" to me. I am sorry if I failed you somehow in being so inaccessible that you felt you could not tell me anything; especially this.

I must go for now. If you want to reply to this letter that is fine. If not then I will wait for a time when you feel less threatened, less vulnerable, less bad about yourself.

All the best
Bro

Letter 2 –
Dear Brother Mark

Dear Mark:

It is still a difficult time for me coming to terms with who you are and what kind of relationship we can possibly ever have in the future. On a suppressed level, I simply find it all interesting or remarkable but mind boggling – and that is on the good days. On other days it is like a tragic news item keeps flashing across the TV in my mind. You know how the news media likes to put almost irrelevant info into a news flash, like age and race? "A fifty-five-year-old white male of Gary, Indiana is convicted of 300 counts of raping his teenage daughter. This is a publicly stirring case," says the pretty young reporter standing in front of the camera with a big microphone pressed to her lips. "Some are calling for a death sentence, some call for castration; some call for both, but there is no one sitting on the fence of ambivalence." In the news flash I see you walking out of a huge courthouse down a long wide set of stairs in handcuffs with head bowed, led by police to a curbside paddy wagon. I can't seem to shake this newsreel that keeps flashing in front of me day and night.

Recently while trying to shake that image I was

dragged into thinking of the World Trade Center towers crashing to the ground in New York City in 2001 and how many times it flashed in front of the entire world, in front of me, and how it is burned into my memory and then I remembered that you phoned me as the first tower was burning, before it collapsed. We were bonded, both gobsmacked and speechless. We watched the smoke, the terror, with our phones pressed hot to our ears, stunned. And now as I sit here 99% recovered from that event, I realize that you might have just pulled yourself off of your teenage daughter to watch that devastation; pulled your hard dick from her young petrified vagina, standing hard in front of the TV.

You might have just raped your daughter and had no idea the degree of devastation that you were in the midst of causing, or maybe you did know. For all I know, you might have thought that you were making love. You might have thought that it was wonderful and tender. I have no idea what you were thinking but you might have thought that you were having a gentle intimate relationship with your daughter but you were indeed actually the World Trade Center towers crashing to the ground; you just did not know it then. You did not know that your life, her life, my life, all of our dear family's lives, and more, were actually in slow motion freefall crashing to rubble, burning.

It has taken years for your crash to happen and the dust to settle, and now the cleanup is hopefully beginning. The Twin Towers took hours to crash and burn, for the dust to settle and for all of the victims to be counted, it took weeks, months and still its aftershock is rippling through fragile minds as post-traumatic stress disorder – PTSD. It took five years for the new building to be erected, finished in 2006 but still the ripples of PTSD are being felt. Sadly, so sadly, I am afraid that your crash and burn, for your raped daughter, for your un-raped daughter, for your other victims, including those who simply liked and loved you and trusted you, it will take much more time to heal for all concerned than simply removing tower rubble.

The newsreel still flashes in front of me, brother; the handcuffs digging into your wrists, your puffy red eyes staring at your feet. Tears of fear dripping to the cold concrete stairs, salt stains of regret – regret that you did what you did, raped your daughter for years, or regret that 'she threw me under the bus when she told her boyfriend'; a quote from you, brother. Which regret do you have, brother? Which are you most afraid of?

This is what I need to know from you, brother, before we can have any kind of relationship. Are you full of remorse for what you did, angry at yourself for fucking your daughter for six years or do you still feel like you have been thrown under the bus by your daughter because she divulged the horrific acts to her boyfriend? This is the hinge brother, the crux of your possible redemption. You have to figure out what it is you are sorry for. Phone me when you are ready to tell me.

Bro

Letter 3 –

Dear Brother Mark

Dear Mark:

The sky is gray today, the heavy under-belly of clouds hangs low like my mood. It is trying to rain. There is little to no wind to stir the branches that hang over our back deck. The bird feeder is busy with thrashing blue jays tossing seed to the ground as they greedily flail for choice, black sunflower seeds with little regard for others. Everything else tossed to the ground. A coo of mourning doves flutters casually to the ground pecking at the spilled seed in the belly-high grass, undisturbed by the chaos of blue that rustles overhead, the recipients of their flailing.

I was thinking that this would be a great photography day. Moody skies dragging through tree tops. For a moment I was wishing that you were here with me to go for a walk to the edge of the lake and shoot the lapping shores like we have done so many times in the past. Whenever I have a question about photography, I instinctively reach for the phone to ask you about aperture settings, f-stop, shutter speed, ISO. You are, in so many ways, the smart one of the two of us. You always have been, brother. You just seem to know stuff. I have always said that you are a smart guy. You are a smart guy about all kinds of stuff like computers and computer programs. It is way easier for me to phone you and get an answer than to look anything up and read and read and figure stuff out. I have always wished I was as smart as you, bro. As you know I am dyslexic, reading has always been difficult and slow for me.

I have often thought what personality trait I would trade with you to be a good, fast reader? Now that I know the truth about you and who you really are and what you are capable of, what you have done with your life, that it turns out that you were, are, a pedophile, a rapist how is it that I could possibly trade any part of who I am for a part of you. Which part of you might I end up with? I will simply be happy being who I am. There is no point in bargaining with the devil. He will always have something up his sleeve. What bargain did you make with the devil? What part of you did you swap for a sexual thrill?

Bro

Email 1

to Michael from Harrison

Dear Michael:

My mind is not in a swirl with the idea that a person can be evil. We have all seen movies or even met the individual that we think is a chronic, psychopathic animal where they are all bad with not a glimmer of hope for redemption. What my mind swirls with is the how? How does the light and the dark live in one person, in the same mind, contemporaneously? How is it that the light shines so brightly and then the Mr. Hyde erupts into the mythical scream in the night?

Harrison

Email 2
to Michael from Harrison

Dear Michael:

I sit here and contemplate what I have done wrong in my life? As perfect and as high and mighty as I might think I am, I look at the moral infractions I have committed and wonder how I might have climbed so high onto the stool of judgment. I shock myself sometimes at how imperfect I was, I am, and maybe I should say, will always be, and now I wonder how can I judge so harshly my dear brother for whom my heart bleeds.

My earliest infraction against a moral code, at least the earliest that I can remember, was when I was only ten. I stole twenty-five cents from my mother's coin box that held the treasury of the small but precious organization for which she was president. The punishment for this crime is that I still remember, more than fifty years later, the anguish that dear mother went through; counting and recounting the fist-full of coins, wondering how she could have miscalculated the tally. With humiliation tucked in the dark recesses between self-incrimination and a sense of stupidity, she turned to father for his calculations and then was finally left to dig in the depths of her handbag for the precious twenty-five cents to make up for her accounting transgression. She prayed that her error would not be recalculated one day by some officious treasurer.

I know that this crime of stealing a single coin might seem insignificant to my greater crimes but one fact that I know is that it sent me on the slippery slope of thinking that I could not only get away with an immoral indiscretion but that I could be absolved of my guilt through time. What was my dear brother's first crime against morality that let him slip into the pit in which he now surely wallows?

There is an important axiom that one needs to keep in mind about the slippery slope. Once you are on the slope, it is infinitely more difficult to gain your footing and climb up than it is to slip further down. Proud of my accomplishment as a thief, it became easy to graduate to bigger booty and even transverse from one moral indiscretion to another; for instance from theft to sexuality.

All the best,
Harrison

Therapy Excerpt –
800 Years of Temptation

Mark was, as usual, slumped in the therapist's green wing-back chair. He was getting tired of hunting and searching for meaning in the past. He was tired of the pain of looking at the history of his life. Breaking a long silence, the therapist leaned forward and said with a whisper of annoyance, "I keep hearing rationalizations from you. I think that you could convince yourself of just about anything and then try to convince me.

"Do you know the story 'The Garden of Paradise' by Hans Christian Andersen? Even though it was written in 1838 it was written just for you. Basically it is a story about temptation, but more importantly that temptation is laced with rationalization. Just like in his case the rationalizations finally failed, as rationalizations always do, in the end you will kiss the tears of the fairy of paradise and then pay the price. In this act of disobedience to a promise, breaking a moral code, you too will be condemned to 800 years of temptation repeating your failures, time and time and time again. Until after all of those wretched years you finally learn, inch by inch by inch, how to overcome temptation.

"You can read the beginning of the story yourself but

basically the crux of it is that the prince is told by the fairy of paradise that she is going to lay down and sleep under the tree of the knowledge of good and evil and the prince is not to even approach her, and to never kiss her no matter the rationalization that comes to him. She told the prince that even if she calls for him, to never come, even to her side. Even if she beckons him to kiss her that he should never, no matter what, never kiss her. The prince is warned that he will be filled with temptation to disobey but be warned that if he does kiss her the garden of paradise will sink into the earth, and the prince will be lost. The prince shrugged and assured the fairy that he would resist all temptation.

"Well basically as the story moves on, the prince was weak and soon found himself rising on one elbow from his sleep just to peek over at the fairy. After all what harm could possibly come of just one peek at her from a distance? Soon he was peeking for the second, third and fourth time and then as he was sitting up and leaning on the tree the prince thought, 'What harm could possibly come from me sitting and watching her at least just to make sure that she is safe.' After a while of watching to make sure she was safe, he heard her calling 'Come, come to me I am in danger.' Little did he know it was just the wind whispering through the branches. He reminded himself that he should not approach her, but just to make sure that it was not her calling, he stood and rationalized that he should listen a bit closer just to make sure. One step closer, two, three just to hear and see that she was safe and then he found he was standing over her arguing with himself that he will not be tempted to kiss her. I have not broken my vow not to kiss her, he argued to himself, 'I am safe to stay and simply admire her beauty but I will not, I must not go any closer.' As he stood over her inching closer and closer, a tiny tear formed in the corner of the eye of the fairy. It glistened like a diamond. It was so beautiful, he thought that he would only get closer to take a look at it. 'I will only look,' thought the prince, but a pure sense of joy filled him. Temptation, and then resistance, and then finally again temptation flooded over him even as he bowed just to look. 'I will not kiss her,' he rationalized, 'but I will only kiss the tear.' As he pressed his lips to the side of her eye he lingered only on the tear for an eternity and then finally felt her sweet skin on his lips and finally, ever so gently kissed her. As he pulled away a clap of thunder, loud and terrible, resounded through the trembling air. All around him fell into ruin. The lovely fairy, the beautiful garden, sunk deeper and deeper. The prince saw it sinking down in the dark night till it shone only like a star in the distance beneath him. Then he felt a coldness, like death, creeping over him; his eyes closed, and he became afraid.

"When he recovered, a chilling rain was beating down on him, and a sharp wind blew across his face. 'Alas! What have I done?' he screamed to the sky. 'I've sinned like Adam, and the garden of paradise has sunken into the earth.' He stood up and found himself in the depths of despair realizing that he had succumbed to temptation, inch by inch, inch by inch, with his ill-fated rationalization. He was now condemned to 800 years of temptation repeating the test of resistance over and over again until he finally mastered to never give in to temptation even for an inch."

Therapy Excerpt –
Mother

"So today it's going to be about my mother is it? Whatever you say. I had an ok relationship with my mother. It wasn't great but she was an ok mother. What more would you like to know? Like I told you once, she used to hound me about my clothes being too gray and my skin was too pale and I should go outside to play in the sun with other kids but mostly she just left me to my own devices while she drank with her sister, my Aunt Mary. The two of them used to drink straight gin with ice because it looked like water so no one knew if they were drinking or drinking. They both put on bright red lipstick and painted their nails bright red and polished off half a bottle in no time.

"One nice thing that I remember about my mom is that she used to read to me when I was little; my dad never did. All he ever read was the TV guide. My mom used to read mostly little kids books from when I was just a toddler and grew into reading more advanced books as I got older. The last book she ever read to me was 'The Prince and the Pauper'. She noticed that I was actually reading along and I was waiting for her to turn the page and she stopped and told me to finish the bloody book on my own and pushed it at me. I think that she was dyslexic and a slow reader and when she discovered that I could read faster than her, she was embarrassed and decided that I could read by myself from then on.

"Before she stopped reading to me she used to read 'The House at Pooh Corner'. She read it to me over and over again. She used to call me her Christopher Robin and rub the top of my head but I didn't like that much because Christopher Robin, in the story, has to grow up and leave Pooh and Piglet and Eeyore and move away and go to school and never see them again. I made her read some chapters so many times that I had memorized the words and I would say them out loud while she was reading. I never let her read that last chapter a second time. It just made me sad.

"I bought that same Christopher Robin book just a few years ago when I saw it in a used bookstore. I haven't read a single word; all I have ever done is look at the pictures. One day I am going to find my own 'Hundred Acre Wood', if you know what I mean. I am going to finally find my place.

"So basically I have that memory of my mom and then there is this other memory that keeps creeping in that I wish I could just forget. One time when my mom and dad were having a big blow out she took me to stay at a motel out of town for about two weeks. She was so determined not to get found by my dad we didn't go to Aunt Mary's place like we sometime used to. I don't know why she left Harrison and Jimmy with my dad, maybe because they were older and could take care of themselves, but basically she packed a bag for me and told by brothers that Dad would be home soon and stay there watching TV. We got in the car and drove outa' town. I guess she had a boyfriend and that is why they were having a fight and she was running away because he used to come over to the motel late at night when they thought that I was sleeping. They would turn the TV on kind of loud and go in the bathroom and have sex. I knew what they were doing. Sometimes they left the bathroom door open a crack and I saw them naked and screwing, her bent over the bathroom sink and him pounding at her from behind. I guess the TV was supposed to drown out their moaning. They would have a shower together and be in there screwin' for an hour.

"In one way it kind of made me sick and angry that he was just fucking my mother and that is all he came for but I never said anything. I got turned on watching them fuck like animals even though I was just little. It turned me on that I was watching something they didn't know that I was watching. I remember thinking that he had a little dick compared to my dad.

"My mom and dad used to screw mostly on Saturday afternoons. I knew they were going to be doing it because they would tell us boys to turn off the TV in the middle of our program and we had to go outside and play. You could hear my dad talkin' dirty through the heat vents and the bed bangin' against the wall. They would go at it for only about ten minutes and then dad would come out all puffed up and smilin' with a clean shirt on and go to the bar for the rest of the afternoon. Aunt Mary would come over and they would get to sippin' gin.

"And that is about it about my mom. I've got other memories about my mom and the family, and shopping and stuff like that but those are the two memories about my mom that kind of sum up my relationship with her. She was kind and gentle and nice to me when I was little and she screwed around on my dad a few times but I figured that he deserved what he got for all the screwing around that he did. Mostly she was an ok mom.

"I am just happy that my mother never knew what kind of a person I really was. Apparently no one ever told mother and apparently Rachel told everyone not to tell her Grandma about what had happened. I am not sure why. I think that it is because Rachel loved me and didn't want to hurt me by telling her grandma.

"Yah I guess my mother loved me the way I was or rather the way that I let her think that I was. I guess that is what mothers do."

Therapy Excerpt –
Thanksgiving

"You have asked me about my mother and father, asked about Frank, my brother, my wives but you have never asked about my old girlfriend Jan. She was just about the only gal that I was interested in for more than just sex. I had a strange conversation with her before we drifted apart. I don't know if she was fishin' for an 'I Love You' or what, but she looked me square in the eye and said, 'Mark, have you actually ever really been in love before?' I was a bit taken aback because we had never talked about love before and I am not sure that I wanted to. What is the point of talking about love? You are or you aren't I figure but at any rate she pushed me for an answer.

"I told her that my first wife, Rose, and I loved each other but we never actually said those three words. It started out as a kind of game. Kind of like who's going to hang up first when you're dating and swooning over spending every minute with the person. She didn't want to say it until I said it and I didn't want to say it until she said it first because I knew she was playing this silent game of who speaks of love first. I think that I loved her. I wrote I L O V E Y O U ! ! in one letter per square on the toilet paper one time and rolled it back onto the roll just to see if she would notice and what her reaction would be. She never said anything. To this day I don't know if she just wiped her toosh with it and didn't notice or what. How could she not notice bright red letters, big letters, one on each square? I wasn't going to ask if she saw the letters or not so to this day I've got no idea. Maybe all she saw was E YOU.

"Even on our wedding night all I could say was 'love yah' and all she said was 'right back at yah.' It's kind of like how I was raised. I don't ever remember my mom or my dad saying 'I love you,' or even 'love yah' to me or my brother for that matter. I can hear my mom saying – 'You don't need to say such things with words. I say "I love you" every time I wash your underwear and cook your dinner. You think I do that because I hate you? Don't be a bone head.' I can remember her waving her spoon at me. 'You don't need smooshy words, you need actions.'

"I know I loved Ruthie, my third wife. She was a nice girl in a lot of ways even if she turned into a nagging bitch but I never told her either. That might be part of why she fucked all those guys behind my back, just to hear someone say, 'I love you'.

"I was at my girlfriend's parent's place for a Thanksgiving dinner about a year ago. I never smelled anything like it before. The aroma of roast turkey, mashed potatoes and yams greeted Jan and me as we walked into the warm house. Like I've told you, Thanksgiving has never been my favorite time of the year. Holidays in general have always been filled with some level of consternation almost all of my life except for when I was little and didn't pay much attention to the fighting. I just can't fathom the mythical harmony that apparently revolved around some dining room tables and post-dinner antics. Telling stories, laughing over spilled milk, playing charades until you had a side-splitting stitch was not part of my family experience. At the very most, my family would watch a football or hockey game with a case of beer, or three. The men would get drunk and argue until they fell asleep. The women would take one car and drive us kids home. The men would show up in the middle of the night, chauffeured by the least drunk of them all.

"Even though I was not all that eager to go, Jan, wanted me to finally meet the rest of her family. Jan and I had been seeing each other steady for five, almost six months and I had managed to avoid spending what she would call, family time, with her parents, brothers and sisters. We arrived early and no one else had shown up yet. Jan is so nice. She put her arm around me and gently dragged me into the kitchen to meet her mom. After an awkwardly stiff hug, a short but polite exchange, it was suggested that I hang out in the family room for a while. 'I'm going to be with mom, helping in the kitchen.'

"Well that's about the end of the story really. I mulled around the posh but friendly family room. I sat and bounced up and down in a large cushioned armchair. I had never sat in such a nice chair before. The house was pretty nice. I just kind of perused all of the original paintings. Some of them were pretty nice. It wasn't till I was looking at all of the books that filled an expansive built-in wall cabinet that surrounded a large bay window that I knew Jan and I were not going to be together very much longer. She came from highbrow stock and I came from common people. It's like she grew up drinking champagne and I grew up drinking cheap beer or wine out of a box.

"I stopped and studied the photographs that paraded the fireplace mantel. It was crazy, I was flooded with memories, though very different from the history beaming from the smiling faces that stared back at me through the silver and black lacquered frames. I realized right then that I had no pictures of my daughters even taped to my fridge. Smiling faces of my estranged daughters only make me depressed. The few family pictures that my family might have are concealed deep in dusty disorder at the bottom of a cupboard somewhere in my aunt's not so family, family room.

"I never really thought of it before but my family memories were more aptly linked to unscrewing the top from the third bottle of cheap wine, glugged by my father into mother's chipped, coffee-stained mug. I started to think maybe Jan and I wouldn't even last another date. Unlike her group-hug-holiday-snapshots, memories in front of a glistening bronze turkey poised for carving, mine were of my father passing me a smoldering joint and telling me to take it into the other room to mommy.

"My Thanksgiving memories were not of family bliss, jokes told around the dining room table, 'pass the gravy' and 'more pumpkin pie anyone?' My Thanksgiving memories were of shattered plates slipped from trembling, inebriated fingers, stacks of unwashed dishes and squabbles over who was going out for fish and chips and another bottle of wine from Joe's wine shop beside the tattoo parlor. My memories were not framed in silver, tastefully placed on a mahogany mantel. Mine were framed in shame, guilt and fear, tucked away in the dark recesses of avoidance, glazed in anger.

"The longer I stayed at Jan's parents' place the weirder

I felt. I pondered the photos, one after another and picked one up to bring it closer. By then I was just sad. It was of a kindly, wrinkled old lady, smiling through the dappled shadows of a white sunhat. She had gentle wide eyes, an arm full of tulips pressed to her chest. For me it was unfathomable that this was a real person and not an image clipped from a magazine.

"Jan walked in the room and said, 'That's my Nanna. She's the one that died about 10 weeks ago. I am sad that you didn't get to meet her. She was such a darling. I miss her so much. I used to stay overnight at her house when I was a little girl.' Jan took the photograph from me, smiled and placed it back precisely where it had come from.

"It made me sad to think that I had no photographs of the only grandmother that I knew. There may be some in a family photo album somewhere. I have no memories of what she looks like. I called my grandma, 'G'. G for grandma. She was kind but distant. She was firm, rather than friendly. She was my only grandmother.

"I got ticked off at Jan when she offered me a glass of wine. I said, 'Why would you offer me a glass of wine when you know that I don't drink anymore?' And then she offered for me to go in the kitchen with her if I wanted to peel potatoes or I could just turn on the TV and see if there was a game on. She reminded me that her dad would not get home from golf with Denis and Deb for an hour. I guess I was just feeling weird or something because I made some comment about me watching a stupid game and I didn't play golf or something stupid like that.

"I just reached for the remote control, grabbed a cushion and stretched out on the long sofa bewildered by the mystery of family bliss. I sat there for a while without the TV on wondering how different my life would have been if I had grown up in such a family with a sofa, uncluttered, untattered and the peace of mind to relax uninterrupted. What would my life be like if I was the one coming home from golf with a dad who cared? What would my life be like if I was the one to have a smiling, doting grandmother and a mother cooking a turkey?

"I sat there alone thinking. I knew that in the long run, one can only blame your past so much for the pain of the present. I guess I was not willing to look at the past, the present or the future with Jan. I kind of screwed up and let her go."

Therapy Excerpt –
Peanut Butter and Banana Sandwich

"I had an ok week I guess. I got to see Frank a couple of times for a coffee but other than that nothing earth-shaking happened. I got a letter from my cousin Bobby that kind of fucked with my head for a day or two. I saved reading it until this past weekend. I was kind of afraid of what it might say, so I put it off. I took it with me for a walk when I went down along the Gary boardwalk. You probably know it, west along the lake towards Chicago. I like to get away from the smell of Gary industry.

"Everyone seems to smile with the bounce of joy in their steps when they are down there. It was a beautiful sunny day on Saturday so I packed a sandwich and drink and went for a walk. There were tons of people meandering along with their kids, and boats in the distance listed only slightly in the gentle offshore breeze. It was kind of fun watching the greedy gulls bolt down french-fries tossed by laughing kids.

"I picked a bench that faced the sun, facing the lake. It was so cool sitting down there looking past the boardwalk to the soft-sand beach eating my peanut butter and banana sandwich – I like the bread toasted and it's gotta be white."

An almost smile involuntarily twitched across Mark's face thinking about his favorite childhood food. Sometimes mashed potatoes with lots of butter were his favorite, but they had to be smooth with plenty of milk like Billie's mother used to make – and they had to be hot.

"Well anyway, I swept the last crumbs to the pigeons cooing at my feet and read the letter. You want me to read you the letter? I got it right here." Mark pulled the letter from his shirt pocket and started to read.

Dear Cuz:

I decided to write a letter and lick a stamp because you have not returned any of my emails, maybe for as long as a year or more.

I was going to use the word 'slighted', slighted that you have ignored me but somehow that word has a bit too heavy of a connotation. I like the precision of language but am not sure that one single word will substitute. My computer thesaurus gave me; ignored, neglected, snubbed, disregarded, omitted, spurned – nope – none of them will do on their own because none of them have the concept of caring built into them. Along with feeling slighted, I have a fear of intruding in your life if you truly don't want to talk to me, though I feel disregarded the way one disregards a telemarketer. Most of what I am feeling has to do with my caring for you as a cousin and hoping, trusting that you are well. We have not had an in depth conversation about life and happiness for a long, long time. We used to sit for hours and talk. I miss that, but now I am hearing some nasty rumors floating around the family about you and need to clear them up.

I missed you at the family reunion again this year, though some were glad that you had the good sense to stay away. It was held at Uncle Len's condo, so some of us went swimming. It has been about four years that you haven't come. Some in the family are actually feeling slighted by your absence, but they might not know about the rumor about you and Rachel. For me it's about missing you and hanging out with you like we used to. I miss riding my bike over to your place and then heading to the pond to catch frogs. I miss those days man. Being cousins is more than just sharing a last name, it's not even about blood and being family. It's about trust and being able to talk about anything even if you did something bad.

I guess you probably know that our cousin Drake passed on last year. I miss him loads; our cousin Nancy the year before that, both from cancer. My sadness goes deeper than just missing a person. It might sound like a cliché but it's not about the bond of DNA. I don't mean this letter to be melodramatic, but I feel like I am losing another cousin. We all have people slip through our lives like Jello off a hot tray. Zip, they are gone, and most often it doesn't matter, but the bond of the ones you love is important no matter what they have done.

Another Thanksgiving dinner has been had without you and another Christmas is around the corner. I hope we can get to see each other again before then, before Easter, before next summer, before one of us joins Drake and Nancy. I know we are older now and not about to go frog hunting, but we could get together and just hang out and talk.

I trust you are well. I hope you are happy. I hope to see

you again soon despite anything that you might have done.

I hate to think that I have to come and hunt you down, Cuz. Write me or email me soon.

I love you,

Bob.

Mark gently, almost in slow motion, folded the letter, slipped it back into the envelope and sat silently with his hands on his lap. Mark felt like the silence in the room was going to choke him.

"So what am I supposed to do now? Write him back, or just ignore him? Bobby is a great guy and all, but we've grown apart since our frog-hunting days. It isn't just him that I've grown apart from. I don't see or talk to anyone since they shunned me for what I did with my daughter. Even before that I started to stay away. I was so tired of everyone thinking of me as the poor orphan boy that lost his parents. 'Poor Mark', lost one parent to drink and the other to a stroke.' I heard them talking behind my back like I was different after my parents died.

"The fact is that when my parents were still alive I liked family gatherings, but that was before they all found out about me and my daughter. I used to like family parties. I even liked helping my mom in the kitchen making pumpkin pies for Thanksgiving feasts. I liked visiting Gram's house with twenty-five or thirty people all showing up with fresh buns and butter, squash, yams, cakes and pies. I liked squeezing in beside cousins, aunts and uncles, plates on our laps, bumping elbows. I kinda liked the fact that the women would be in the kitchen doing women stuff. I liked the tradition of the men hooting and hollering, gathered around the TV watching the Orange Bowl even if they were half cut and I liked rabble-rousing with my cousins in the basement. I liked everything, even if my dad drank too much and my uncles argued about hunting and gun control and too many trucks on the highway.

"I remember one year we swiped the blankets from all of the beds to make forts between the tables and chairs in the basement. It was like an elaborate maze zigzagged through the entire big open room. One time we almost burned the place down with a candle one of the girls took into one of the blanket-slumped vaults. Oh man we were shocked back to reality when that happened. We got it out quick and we hid the burned sheet. It was like time stood still for those hours of fun and fantasy, but now they are gone.

"One year, when I was about ten, I was bouncing around the basement on a pogo-stick and banged my head on the low beam that ran down the middle of the room. They called me beam-brain for the rest of that holiday. Every time I walked into the room they would laugh at me and say, 'Duck Mark, duck.' I only half minded. Mostly I just kinda liked the attention, the belonging – but now all that is gone and it is my own fault."

Mark scuffled his feet on the posh gray carpet in front of his chair. "What am I supposed to do?" Mark mumbled to himself rubbing his hands over his face. "How am I supposed to just pick up with Bobby as if it was yesterday? I'm happy just the way I am. I've got Frank and my job. I don't need anyone or anything else."

Letter 4 –

Dear Brother Mark

Dear Mark:

For years, you have been saying that you suffer from depression. I have empathized, sympathized and commiserated. I have felt badly for you and even worried about you committing suicide. I have phoned just to keep your mind occupied. I have sent txt messages with photos and emailed. I have prayed for you. I have offered some not so practical ideas of how you might overcome the effects of depression by sitting in the sun more, jogging more, taking up yoga or Tai Chi. I have suggested that you might change your diet, eat less carbs, eat less meat, eat less sugar, less salt, more sleep, all to no avail.

I have suggested to different people that they call you just to make sure you are alright and are not about to jump in front of a train, and now I wonder how much of your depression is simply symptomatic of being a pedophile for years. When did you start being depressed? I don't want to suggest that all depression is linked to being a pedophile or that everyone that suffers from depression will become or has been a pedophile. But man it must really fuck with your head, but maybe it doesn't affect you at all. Maybe you are just fine with being a pedophile and fucking your daughter for six years, but it sure is fucking with my head. It sure does cause me to be depressed. Numbers of how many times you raped your daughter keep flashing in my mind. It truly is depressing, brother.

I put the Christmas lights up this week. I remember you helping me one year, both of us with frozen fingers because it was colder than usual that year. We always had fun doing stuff like that. It has been a while but after the lights were up, I guess it was a couple of years ago, you said something about being depressed and could not get in the spirit of Christmas. I just fluffed it off. I didn't want to hear anything about it. The lights were up, they were pretty, I was happy and I didn't want to know anything about your depression. For me there was nothing like Christmas lights to take away the blues, but it didn't seem to help you and now I am starting to figure out why. The wrongs that we do in our life are like a marble rattling around in a can. You just can't make it stop rattling no matter what you do. The wrongs that we do in our life just don't go away because we string pretty lights in front of the house.

Before I go I have to say one last thing about how smart you are but you sure are stupid. You use your smarts in all the wrong way. I looked up some stuff on the internet about what you did. The experts say that the reason pedophiles get away with their abuse for so long is that they choose their victims well. It's like you have a homing beacon that lights up when you find a girl that is lonely and neglected and desperate for love, and you found all of those things in your Rachel. You were able to seduce her because you gave her the very things she craved: attention, support, approval, respect and all the other things we associate with love. What I read also says that it works because sex is pleasurable and satisfying, even for a twelve-year-old little girl. It feels good from the inside out. It creeps most people out to think of a pre-pubescent child experiencing sexual pleasure, but they can and do all the time.

I gotta go. I probably said too much already. I hope you've read this over a couple of time and talked to a therapist about it – if you've finally gotten to the point where you're seeing one. I don't want you thinking this is just me talking.

I hope we can talk soon.

Harrison

Therapy Excerpt –
Tick Tick Tick

"Oh man I had a hard night last night. I didn't get much sleep. I lay in bed trying to read. Like I have told you, it is my habit to read myself to sleep these days with a box of Kleenex within arm's reach, but last night there was a distant tick tick tick that distracted my concentration. I rustled loudly as I turned the pages of my book just to make some noise so I couldn't hear the tick tick and then I frumpt my pillow and smoothed the sheets, all in an attempt to distract myself. I was reading 'Lolita', by Vladimir Nabokov but I sat up and visually perused the room for the frickin' tick, tick, tick. I couldn't figure out where the noise was coming from. I even talked to, Albert, my made-in-China, imitation English, white, green-eyed ceramic cat that was given to me when grandma 'G' passed on years ago.

"Eventually I found the ticking. I slipped the culprit watch into my top dresser drawer and returned to my book.

"By the way I don't want you to get the wrong idea about me reading 'Lolita'. It's not because it is particularly salacious or anything like that. I read it because it was on the 'TIME magazine's' list of the 100 best English-language novels and Ralph from work said it was a famous book from the mid-50s and it was a good read.

"Even after I put the watch in the drawer I still couldn't read myself to sleep even though I was tired. I kept on thinking about Rachel and how she is still carrying the brunt of this sex stuff and I wished she was more like Lolita and just enjoyed it and didn't get all fucked-up about it. If she is not careful she will carry it for the rest of her life. I was thinking about Lolita and she was just eleven when she was having sex with, Humbert. Humbert, weird name for a weird guy. He was the protagonist of the story, a thirty-eight year-old, literature professor and he liked young girls that he called 'nymphets'.

"I never finished the book because it got boring but I wondered if Lolita was going to suffer a thousand times more like Rachel is, or at least that is what I figure she is suffering because she won't talk to me. In the book, it is suggested that Lolita will always question what love is and how to express it. Because Humbert was having sex with Lolita way younger than I was with Rachel I figure that she will probably even doubt the existence of love. Like Rachel, will Lolita be confused about sex and love for the rest of her life? Even with therapy. I hate to speculate about Lolita and Rachel. I figure that they will make it just fine if everyone just treats them normal instead of broken."

Therapy Excerpt –

The Top Drawer

"Everything's ok with me I guess. I'm not sleeping any better. One night when I couldn't settle down I was poking around in the top drawer of my dresser looking for a packet of matches from the bar that a buddy and I went to a few weeks ago. As I was rummaging I wondered if everyone had a top dresser drawer of socks that was also a catch-all for the minutiae of life, you know what I mean, the bits and pieces that have nowhere else to go. Does everyone have a three-year-old chestnut – dried and puckered; a few matchbox cars – scratched and worn from when they were five-years' old? Some of them have pink dots on the bottom and it reminded me of when I was little that all three of us boys would get cars for Christmas or birthday and my mother would put a pink fingernail polish dot on the bottom of mine and a red dot on the bottom of Jimmy's but Harrison, because he was older and didn't play with dinky toys much, his had no dots. This color code was to stop us from fighting over whose car was who's. We never really learned how to share. I was thinking about cleaning out that top drawer and then thought, not likely. Rearrange maybe but toss anything that is as important as a braided bracelet that Rachel gave me when she was just ten, or the handmade Father's Day card with a stick man picture of me standing between my two daughters.

"I figured it would be emotional suicide if I even looked too deep into the drawer let alone threw something out. Somehow even the dust and disorder were an important part of what I began to think of as a growing, ever-changing time-box; a walk down the memory lane of better times.

"Well I mumbled and rummaging for a few minutes and finally pulled out a movie ticket stub from one of my last dates with Ruthie. I paused and remembered the gentle times I had with her holding hands in the dark of the flickering theatre.

"What could I have done to make her love me more, to desire to keep our oath of 'til death do us part.' I just got angry and refused to lament so I jammed the ticket stub back in under the socks and closed the drawer. I figured no pain or pleasure is ever lost from one's top dresser drawer unless you let it escape, so I closed it and didn't go into it, even for socks, for days. The desire to find that girl's phone number on the back of the matches just evaporated. I figured that I would rather sit at home with Ruthie rattling in my brain than feign interest in someone who was likely only going to be a one-night-stand. Sometimes it just has to be ok to take a painful walk down memory lane.

"I figured I must be getting old or something. That was the first time that I ever turned down the possibility of a one-night stand. I sat at home that evening and was starting to realize that there was just no relevance to my concept of time and history. It is all too painful. Time for me was like vegetable soup – all the little bits of my history were mixed up in the pot of pain, indistinguishably bubbling, gurgling away in a steaming cauldron of existentialism. For me it was hard to dip in and grab just one memory that I was happy to recount. I argued with Frank that there is no such thing as time if you don't have memories. It doesn't stand still, it doesn't zip by. It just doesn't exist. Well I know that my arguments did not really stand up to scrutiny but I just did not know how to cope with the fact that I had no real fond memories of anything. A sliver of time, one slice at a time can evaporate into the hidden, repressed memories that are lost in the pot of soup we call life.

"I just don't remember much from my past. I just kind of shut out time and history. Frank tells me all kinds of stories about his childhood, so I adopted them all. I tell colleagues at the office about the years of going to my family cottage on Lake Michigan – Frank's cottage, Frank's memories, about his dad's bantam chickens in the shed behind his stucco house – Frank's dad's chickens, Frank's memories, his large sandbox, arguing with his brother over dinky toys – whose cars were whose – all his memories. I told them about finding a few of those dinky toys in my top drawer just the other day. He has told me so much about his great childhood that his stories started to become my bits of memories to cherish. Those slivers of memories actually became mine. I was having lunch with the guys from the office last week and they were telling each other stories about their childhood. One guy from Sri Lanka telling us about his granny and her cooking and everyone eating together. Another guy talked about a pony he had and loved. I started to tell them about my years on the farm north of Chicago, along the lake and the big gray old barn we had there, but you and I know those were Frank's memories – not mine. I told them all about my marvelous childhood and the duck pond. The only time that I can actually remember events is when I find an object that triggers a memory. Do you have a top dresser drawer full of hidden memories?

"I couldn't think of anything fun or interesting to tell them about my life. It's full of fuck-ups. All I could remember were the years I lived in the basement apartment with my mom after my dad left us. I slept with my mom except when she had a guy over and then I slept on the floor beside the fridge with my feet under the table so I wouldn't get stepped on. There was no room in the little bed that Harrison and Jimmy slept in. No light streamed into my life for most of those years. It is one of those scenes from a movie – my dad went out for cigarettes and never came back, but I sure didn't want to tell them that. I was getting ready to tell them about me / Frank's bicycling to the reservoir and building a fire to cook hotdogs, but it was time for us to get back to our desks. Like the fraud I am I skulked back to my desk and pretended I was happy pushing papers. You don't even know the half of what I skulk about, and you never will. No matter how many therapy sessions we have."

Email to Family from Harrison –
December 27

Dear All:

It is 8am, the morning after our family Christmas party. With blurry eyes, after a 5-hour drive home and a good night's sleep, I am compelled to start writing this post-Christmas letter.

First – Helen – you will be glad that I stole the book, "Edward Lear's Book of Nonsense" from you from the present game. Here are two highlights from the book.

'There was a Young Lady whose eyes,
Were unique as to color and size;
When she opened them wide,
People all turned aside,
And started away in surprise.'

I will only inflict a second one on you.

'There was an Old Man who supposed,
That the street door was partially closed;
But some very large rats,

Ate his coats and his hats,
While that futile old gentleman dozed.'

I have to admit that I chuckled from cover to cover last night. I am sure I will find a twelve-year old with a bizarre sense of humor who will enjoy it.

I wanted to say how great it was to see everyone yesterday, though obviously sad that some were missing.

Cindy, thank you for the meat balls that you containered especially for me to take home. I had some at the party and they were great as usual. Thanks. The best spice of all is your spice of generosity. Thanks for all of the presents that you added to the present game. It was lots of fun as usual.

As our family newsletter said, "It is great to be on the right side of the grass with you all." Richard and I sat together quite a bit at the family party. I learned the true meaning of that saying from him – thanks. Over the years he has always joyously said to me when I asked how he was doing, "I am on the right side of the grass and that's what counts." I am glad to share turkey with you all – thanks Betty for bringing the turkey, stuffing, etc.

Our dearest Selene, I am sorry you were brought to tears at the Christmas party thinking of your dad and how sad he is for missing family at this time of year. I tried to say in a few words; I am not at all sad that he is sad. This has to be part of his spiritual growth process, his penance. Only in his aloneness will he suffer the consequences of his actions and this is a supremely good thing. I learned very late in life, I am still learning, the axiom that there are consequences for all of our actions. Big and small actions have big and small consequences. Generosity of love was not his action. He must pay the price that others are and will, for possibly a long time, suffer for his actions. Thank heavens we do not live in a society that believes in stoning. Family shunning is a small price to pay for his actions. Each of us are dealing with forgiveness, in our own way, at our own speed. Thank goodness divine Love still loves him. We will all arrive at the same place of forgiveness sooner or later, this life or next.

Jane, Rachel and Paul, we all missed you. We love you. It is only half of a party when not all of the family can be there.

Aside from the food, the presents, the chatter, the hugs, the highlight of the party, for me, was driving Lionel around in circles on his great-grandma's scooter. Can you still hear the squeals of joy reverberating in the foyer? I know some of you took pictures, can you send one to all of us?

Happy New Year, everyone.
Harrison

A Phone Call From Frank –
And Never Coming Back

Hello Mark, Frank here.

Mark, how you doin'? What's up?

I got your email saying you were going away and never coming back. I figured it was a joke and I just didn't get around to sending a reply. It sounded way too cryptic for me to just email back.

What do you mean you are or you aren't? You are going away and you aren't coming back? What's that mean? Whe're you going? Surely you are coming back eventually even if only to visit.

No! What do you mean no?

Ok, ok I got it. You're leaving and you're never coming back. Where are you going? Can I come and see you sometime?

What do you mean, No?! Well eventually. No as in never or no as in you don't know when?

Ok, ok I got it. You're leaving and you're never coming back and I can't come to visit you, or at least you hope not for a very long time from now. Email? How about email, can I still email you?

Mark you are starting to scare me. Where are you going that you won't have email?

Ok, ok. You won't have a computer but there are internet cafés. Set up a Yahoo or Hotmail account before you go and I'll email you if or when you get to a computer some time.

No email. Ok, ok no email. Where the hell are you going, the Antarctic with a dog team for the rest of your life or a monastery? Where are you going anyway? Why all the secrecy for frickin' sakes? When are you leaving?

You don't know exactly but you know you are going soon and you can't tell me where and I can't email you? Sounds pretty bloody cryptic to me. If you change your mind email me and...

Ok, ok no email but what the hell man? I've known you for 28 years and you're just dropping off the face of the earth and you can't tell me anything. You are scaring me for sure now, Mark. Trouble; are you in some sort of trouble? Maybe I can help. What's the problem? Money? I'll send you some money. How much do you need? Money makes all problems disappear.

You don't need any money where you're going? No email, no money, I presume no snail mail or phone. Where are you going? Shangri-La? If you don't need money and you can't have email, you might as well be dead, man. Come on, man, give me a hint.

I love you too man! What's with all of the sappy I love you stuff anyway? Are you going to be home for a while? I will come right over tomorrow after work.

Cold Steel

The first line from 'Metamorphosis', by Franz Kafka, is: "As Gregor Samsa woke one morning from a troubled dream…"

As Mark woke one morning from a troubled dream he swung his legs over the coffee table, stumbled past the kitchen and made his way to the bathroom. Holding the door jamb he groped his way to consciousness. Early morning glared in the speckled bathroom mirror blinding him to the bloodshot, talcum complexion that squinted back. Rubbing the back of his neck he leaned forward straining to see his reflection. With trepidation he paused, wondering if he would see the metamorphosed exoskeleton of Gregor Samsa. As he slowly came into focus he was morbidly delighted to see his own gray, eye-sunken image staring back at him.

A full night on the sofa after reading Franz Kafka's "Metamorphosis" is enough to give anyone a paralytic kink in the neck, he thought after rolling his head from side to side. In his stumbling stupor he could hardly figure out what was dream and what was reality; what was a spillover from the terrifying book he still had rattling in his mind. Elbows on knees, he sat painfully, slowly releasing, waiting, for the flow of relief.

Stepping out from his pajama bottoms he shuffled

down the laundry strewn, picture-less hall. Hands on both walls he fumbled his way to the bedroom. Flopping on his unmade bed he covered his head with his stained, pillowcase-less pillow. Within seconds Mark was stirring in fretful sleep, once again, staring down Kafka's giant beetle wondering if it would run from him or attack with its pincered claws. Standing on its hind legs, it stared eye to eye at Mark breathing the hot, rotting stench of hell in his face. Pincers rattled rhythmically, nervously twitching like a drunken butcher scything the air with a fist full of knives. Poised, motionless, Mark stared deep into the creature's bloodless eyes searching for his strength to stay calm. Cold sweat streamed from his terrified face; muscles ached with throbbing fear. He could see his own reflection in the shimmering shell of his nemesis. As it raised a silver claw slowly to his face he could see the cockroach had his same drawn and tired features, the same gray, sunken eyes. It stroked his face with cold steel, his teary glass eyes.

Mark jolted back to life. Sitting on the side of his bed, Mark wiped the sweat from his brow. He stared at a new hole in his sock. His untrimmed big toenail had scissored its way into open air. "I'm fuckin' pathetic," he said out loud to himself. "You aren't even motivated enough to cut your own damn toenails let alone get another job or even get rid of the damn raccoon in the backyard. Maybe your shrink isn't as stupid as you think. Stupid cockroach, you deserve every bit of crap that comes your way." Wiggling his toe he leaned over, yanked the sock off of his foot and apathetically threw it across the room at an unruly pile of dirty laundry.

That was the last straw. In that instant Mark

plummeted from depression into the dark depths of hopelessness. He was now more despondent than he thought possible. Three times divorced, stuck in a boring, unsatisfying job – and now a hole in his sock. Mark had slowly, one by one, let friends and social activities drain from his life. The only real friend he had left was Frank, but even Frank now had Dorothy.

Self-pity grew to be his only companion. It grew in Mark like black mold in a petri dish, smothering, eventually filling every crevice of his life. It felt to Mark like life was just not worth living. His discontent was more than the general malaise that had hovered in his life for years. It was now the constant unyielding consternation of self-deprecation. At this moment it seemed there was only one way out.

Mark reached for the revolver that had been sitting conspicuously on his night table for weeks and jammed the cold muzzle into his mouth. Pointing the barrel to the roof of his mouth he pulled gingerly on the trigger and stopped. He toggled the hammer back and forth ever so gently. He wondered just how far he could pull the trigger before the gun would fire and it would all be over. He wondered if anyone would care. Mark gently released the trigger. With muzzle still in his mouth he wiped tears from his eyes and again pulled gently, just a little further this time and again gently released. Pulling the barrel from his mouth he threw the gun violently across the room smashing a lamp before it came to rest in the corner.

Mark collapsed with a heavy sigh into the chair, resigned to his task. He reached for a pen, pulled a note pad from a stack of papers and books that were on his night table. He opened the note pad and waited for the right words.

Dear Mary: I have to take care of this one last thing before I leave. I have to apologize for being such a jerk. I have finally come to a painful realization of just how utterly selfish I am. When I was over at your place last week I took the last slice of the special raisin bread that you like so much. Even though I jokingly offered it around to others with my mock auction – "Going once, going twice, going... too late it's mine." I should not have taken the last piece. Even though I beat myself up over this I realized that I never apologized to you. I can't help it. I tell myself over and over again that it does not have to be me, me, me – I am sorry. It seems that I will never learn – I will never learn. I am sorry. Mark Beatleman.

With precision Mark slowly tears the paper from the pad and with gentle care folds it into quarters. Pressing his hand across the final fold he stands the tented paper like a card on the night table where the gun once sat.

Shuffling to the corner of the room, Mark, kicks the broken lamp out of his way, picks up the flung revolver and sticks the cold steel muzzle back in his mouth. Penetrating the barrel with the tip of his tongue he is shocked by the acidic chemical residue. Sucking air through the barrel he slowly, ever so slowly, with deliberate hesitation pulls the trigger. This time all the way.

– The End 1 –

Postscript

Obviously this ending of my autobiographical story is fiction, I did not pull the trigger and I did not die, though suicide seemed like a tempting option for me at more than one point. My family still won't talk to me, my daughter Rachel hasn't talked to me for years and Selene lets more and more time slip between her phone calls and visits. I am still alive and in moderately good health, though I still suffer from severe bouts of depression. I suffer less and less from the anxiety of more and more people finding out my true story, especially now knowing that this book will be published. I am an open book now. I hoped that if I simply told my story and got it off my chest that I could return to suffering in silence for what I did to my dear daughter. My shrink thinks that me telling my story was about self-punishment but partly I think it was simply cathartic. I was weak enough to do what I did to her but strong enough to not commit suicide – does that make any sense. In the end I figure that I would hurt Rachel even more if I actually did pull the trigger all the way. I have done enough harm. I cannot bear to inflict more.

This alternate ending is the true ending to my story. I truly did wake up on the sofa from reading the book "Metamorphosis" by Kafka.

Alternate Ending –

The Metamorphosis of Mark Beatleman

As Mark woke one morning from a troubled dream he swung his legs over the coffee table, stumbled past the kitchen and made his way to the bathroom. Holding the door jamb he groped his way to consciousness. Early morning glared in the speckled bathroom mirror blinding him to the bloodshot, talcum complexion that squinted back. Rubbing the back of his neck he leaned forward straining to see his reflection. With trepidation he paused, wondering if he would see the metamorphosed exoskeleton of Gregor Samsa. As he slowly came into focus he was morbidly delighted to see his own gray, eye-sunken image staring back at him.

A full night on the sofa after reading Franz Kafka's 'Metamorphosis' is enough to give anyone a paralytic kink in the neck, he thought after rolling his head from side to side. In his stumbling stupor he could hardly figure out what was dream and what was reality. He stopped for a moment and stared at the floor, scratched his head and kicked his revolver down the hall towards the bedroom. Nothing was clear to him. What was a spillover from the terrifying book he still had rattling in his mind and what was the reality of his morose life. Elbows on knees he sat, painfully, slowly releasing, waiting, for the flow of relief.

Stepping out from his pajama bottoms he shuffled down the laundry-strewn, picture-less hall. Hands on both walls he fumbled his way to the bedroom. He stooped and picked up the revolver and flopped on his unmade bed. Revolver still in his hand he covered his head with his stained, pillowcase-less pillow. Within seconds Mark was stirring in fretful sleep, once again, staring down Kafka's giant beetle wondering if it would run from him or attack with its pincered claws. Standing on its hind legs, it stared eye to eye at Mark breathing the hot, rotting stench of hell in his face. Pincers rattled rhythmically, nervously twitching like a drunken butcher scything the air with a fist full of knives. Poised, motionless Mark stared deep into the creature's bloodless eyes searching for his strength to stay calm. Cold sweat streamed from his terrified face; muscles ached with throbbing fear. He could see his own reflection in the shimmering shell of his nemesis. As it raised a silver claw slowly to his face he could see the cockroach had his same drawn and tired features, the same gray, sunken eyes. It stroked his face with cold steel, teary glass eyes. Unflinchingly, it pulled ever so carefully away. Crouched onto all six legs it scampered into the darkness and disappeared.

Mark jolted back to life.

What day of the week is it? Is it a work day or weekend? Mark flicked on the small black and white TV that sat beside his bed hoping to catch the news and a clue. "Saturday. Thank God it's Saturday. What time is it?" Mark stretched for his flung watch. "Great. Saturday and I still have time to meet Frank at Roasters Coffee Shop." Mark smacked his bare belly with both hands a few times enjoying the exhilarating smart. "Saturday. Frank. Pants. Pants, where are my pants? Living room." Dashing down the hall he popped into the bathroom, slapped cold water on his face, rubbed his wet hands back and forth through his hair and decided not to shave. "Ok. Shoes. Shoes. Where are my shoes? Hall, front door." Tucking in his wrinkled shirt he grabbed for his wallet and sprang out the door leaving it unlocked.

A bit out of breath Mark bounded into the almost full Roasters Coffee Shop and glanced around. "Frank, so glad you are still here. How are you doing? You been here long?" He dashed over and, uncharacteristically, gave Frank a quick squeeze; almost hug, on the shoulder. "Can I get you anything? It's my treat. I'll be right back. Hey, Sarah. How are you doing today? You look gorgeous, as usual. Have I ever told you that I love your auburn hair? Give me a Cappuccino today and one of those fruit and nut square thingies, oh and another one of whatever coffee Frank just finished."

"You sound like you are in a good mood today Mark. What's up, win one of those lottery 'scratch and sniffs' that you are always desperately playing? I'll bring your Cappuccino and Frank's coffee over in a minute."

"You know why I am in such a good mood today? Well I won't make you guess. It's because I woke up just twenty minutes ago and found out I'm not a beetle and I'm just good old, fucked-up, Mark Beatleman."

Sarah smiled and smirked at Mark and pushed the plate towards him, "I always knew you weren't Ringo Starr or Harrison Lennon. Glad you finally figured it out."

Mark whisked the plate from the counter and headed back to Frank. "Frank, have you ever woken up from a really realistic dream and found out you weren't dead?"

"What do you mean? I wake up not dead every morning and by the way what the hell was up with that phone conversation the other night? You really fucked with me you bone head."

"Don't worry about that for now. I will explain later but you know what I mean. You have a totally realistic dream. You act out every part of it. Not a minute is missing in the dream. It is so real that you can even remember the smell of things. Everything is in color and you wake up in a sweat and you think you are dead. You are just numb and you think that you are dead and then you slowly realize that you're actually alive and then you start to feel your head throbbing and you are almost glad you have a headache and then you slowly realize you are soaking wet with sweat and you have a really bad taste in your mouth and even that you are glad about because you are starting to realize that you are actually alive and everything is ok, still fucked-up but still ok. You know what kind of dream I mean? I've had smaller dreams like that all the time but less vivid, nothing like this one. I just woke up a half an hour ago from a dream just like that."

Frank puts down his New York Times and leans forward. "No I've never had a dream like that. Sounds dreadful. That might explain why you look like you just fell out of the center of a tornado, but how come you are in such a good mood?"

"Well that's just it, Frank. I'm alive and I'm not a cockroach. Yah I know I've been a cockroach in the past but have you ever read Franz Kafka's book "Metamorphosis"? I don't know what Freud would say about my dream but I've thought I was a cockroach all my life and sometimes I acted like one, but in the end I stared him down and he just skulked away. It was amazing. I dreamed the entire book last night and I turned into a cockroach just like Gregor Samsa and I woke up thinking that I was going to see me, me the cockroach, in the mirror but instead I saw me, my real self, still kinda fucked-up but just me."

From across the table Frank takes a joking swing at Mark, "And that's a good thing?"

"Screw off, yah that's a good thing. I was never so glad to be myself ever in my life. I can't believe it. I'm not a cockroach and I am glad to be me."

Sarah leaned over Mark's shoulder, "Here's your Cappuccino Mr. Lennon and here is your coffee Mr. Starr."

Mark reached up to take the Cappuccino from Sarah. "You're wonderful, lots of foam, just the way I like it, thanks. I should have a Cappuccino more often. Frank, I have to tell you some stuff about me that is going to hurt but I gotta tell you. I gotta tell you now before I lose my nerve."

– The End 2 –

Comment on Ending Two

This is the true ending of the story. I have received letters from anonymous readers, from the first edition of the book, saying that I should have pulled the trigger. Still to this day, on my worst days of remorse, I wonder if they are right. Judge me as you may but that is my life, and it is going to unfold the way it has to, not the way anyone else feels it should. I was a total fuckup for so many years. I raped my daughter and I am sorry and I can't do anything about it now. I don't expect forgiveness but I do still strive for redemption. Life for me now is a renovation project. Fixing all the cracks and peeling paint is an ongoing job.

I do realize that much of the book is written in the perspective that I was right, that society is wrong, that therapy is only psychobabble and the world perspective sucks. I have to admit that had been my perspective for the longest time but it was important to include what I was thinking even though the reality is that, I think, I have reformed and have a truly better understanding of sexual abuse. If this story does not show my true level of redemption that is ok with me. The most important thing for me is to have a future abuser recognize that they have a choice before they do anything that they later regret; self-satisfaction is not the best choice.

Postscript

"Spotlight"

Dear readers of my memoir. As this book is getting ready to go to press the film "Spotlight" is being presented at movie theaters across North America. I must say it is a movie worth seeing. Every sector of society will be shocked. The pedophiles in the audience will be relieved to know that they are statistically not so much of an abnormality as they felt they were. Their shame will not be diminished and they will not be absolved by anyone in the audience, in fact they should not let anyone know of their crimes as they might be lynched before they reach the dark safety of the street for a fast get away.

The movie presents the notion that 50% of all Roman Catholic priests are sexually active and have broken their vow of celibacy and chastity. If breaking the vow of celibacy includes abstinence from masturbation then I would suggest that the numbers are even higher than 50% and there are a lot more liars in the priesthood than anyone might admit. For me the important statistic is that the movie suggests 6% of priests have committed a sexual act with a minor and now the media is suggesting that maybe the percentage is closer to 10% or higher. Totally aside from statistical analyses and debating whether it is 6 or 10% it has to be recognized that there are a lot of pedophile priests out there. The Roman Catholic Church would like to add the idea of "past tense" to that statement. Whether or not it is past tense for the Roman Catholic Church or not the media is dragging up scandal after scandal about sexual abuse committed by hockey coaches, Boy Scout leaders, teachers and the list goes on and on. They are all being dragged into the limelight.

I can't help but wonder how many unreported sex acts with minors there are still out there. I am starting to think that I am not so abnormal. Because of the movie "Spotlight" a ninety-two-year-old man has finally come to the media and reported that 80 years ago he was forced to committed fellatio on his parish priest and had never spoken of it, to anyone, till this day. How many times has a man tickled the fancy of a 12-year-old girl and gotten away with it? How many times at the family picnic has Uncle Harry, "on purpose by accident" brushed up against his teenage niece and copped a feel or made a comment about her growing womanhood. As I contemplate this I am starting to feel absolutely normal. How many times has a fellow-being simply thought it but never committed the act. How many times has an 18-year-old boy living at home with his ten-year old, twelve-year old or even fifteen-year old sister taken advantage of her naiveté and touched her in ways that society would not condone. I am thinking that the numbers might be shockingly high.

My warning to you all is that if you condemn me for my actions and if this movie "Spotlight" teaches you nothing else it should teach you to never, never, absolutely never, trust a man to be alone with an underage child. Let me repeat, "absolutely never". Never trust the priest, the Boy

Scout leader, the coach or the teacher. Never trust the adolescent boy to babysit your daughter or your son. Never trust the police officer, the doctor, the dentist behind closed doors with your underage child. If more than 50% of priests are breaking their holy vow of celibacy after years of training and commitment to God then what percentage of your sexually active males, of any age, would take advantage of the innocence of a little girl or boy if they had a chance. For God sake don't give a prospective pedophile the chance to turn into an abuser.

We are all sexual beings including the adolescent child, girl or boy, looking for a sexual thrill. If you allow a man to be behind closed doors with a child then you are part of the problem.

I still contemplate the idea that every form of sex even with a child is actually a form of love. Even after all of these years of therapy, after my internal debate and the sex that I had with my daughter, I still wonder if it was mutually desired and a shared act of love. This unresolved internal struggle may be the end of me. I will either finally come to a level of acceptance of my acts or I will finally put the muzzle in my mouth and pull the trigger, pulled by the finger of remorse.

Mark Beatleman

Reviews of
Living in the Shadow

It was difficult for me to read this memoir because I know a number of people – some very close, even a relative, that went through years of sexual abuse at the hands of a father, brother or uncle. It is difficult for me because I have only known victims and never the perpetrators – sorry I can't have any forgiveness for those who could do such a thing, especially over time. I know the past is the past and I think that I understand redemption, salvation and forgiveness but the victim will suffer in agony for years. My heart is with the victim not the redemption of the abuser. My emotional side says he should be locked up and sterilized but my Christian upbringing says we should give him every chance to redeem himself. I wonder, is redemption even possible?

**John Bissett,
Fiction writer, "The Veiled Mind of Man"**

Gary, Indiana's, Mark Beatleman, brings you his true life story of sliding down the slippery slope of immorality into the swamp of becoming a sexual predator. At the very least you will grow from his desperate attempt of finding love in all the wrong places. This true confession of pedophilia and incest will touch everyone in one way or another. Every man needs to read this book and be disgusted by the actions of Mark Beatleman.

Josie Whitford,
Gary Indiana Post

Because of my position at Gary Indiana University and teaching Criminal Justice, I hear endless accounts of pedophilia, date rape and physical abuse. I hear about the trauma that the victim will carry for the rest of their lives. Even through the process of forgiveness, even with therapy, it will haunt the abused in the background of their lives forever. Every single day the hurt, the pain will lurk, making them question all things; question the truth of anything. It doesn't go away. I have watched this from the sidelines all too many times to believe the memories of pain will ever fade. I have seen it 'resolved' only to surface years later. Even though this book is a must read for every male, I believe that Mark Beatleman, should have limited options that include little more than castration and/or becoming a cloistered monk.

Bradley Corbett,
Professor, Gary Indiana University
Bachelor of Science, Criminal Justice